THE
MEZZOGIORNO
SOCIAL CLUB

ESSENTIAL PROSE SERIES 137

THE MEZZOGIORNO SOCIAL CLUB

ERCOLE GAUDIOSO

GUERNICA
EDITIONS
TORONTO · BUFFALO · LANCASTER (U.K.)
2017

Michael Mirolla, editor
David Moratto, cover design and interior layout
Cover Photo: Ercole Gaudioso,
Rear of Manhattan Little Italy building
Guernica Editions Inc.
1569 Heritage Way, Oakville, (ON), Canada L6M 2Z7
2250 Military Road, Tonawanda, N.Y. 14150-6000 U.S.A.
www.guernicaeditions.com

Distributors:
University of Toronto Press Distribution,
5201 Dufferin Street, Toronto (ON), Canada M3H 5T8
Gazelle Book Services, White Cross Mills
High Town, Lancaster LA1 4XS U.K.

First edition.
Printed in Canada.

Legal Deposit—Third Quarter
Library of Congress Catalog Card Number: 2017932210
Library and Archives Canada Cataloguing in Publication
Gaudioso, Ercole, author
The mezzogiorno social club / Ercole Gaudioso.

(Essential prose ; 137)
Issued in print and electronic formats.
ISBN 978-1-77183-165-9 (softcover).--ISBN 978-1-77183-166-6 (EPUB).
--ISBN 978-1-77183-167-3 (Kindle)

I. Title. II. Series: Essential prose series ; 137

PS3607.A964M49 2017   813'.6   C2017-900602-9   C2017-900603-7

Dedicated to my brother, Ralphie.
He left us too soon, but managed to sit by my side
whispering in my ear through all the writes and rewrites

Contents

PART ONE

PART TWO

PART ONE

The Farmhouse

In the farmhouse at the edge of the neighborhood, an eighteenth-century oil on canvas hangs above a fireplace. The scene is of the house angled in a clearing squared by woods of chestnut and ash. A little girl at an upstairs window gazes out through a pane of glass that is flared by the sun, but her face sharply reveals anticipation.

A barn overlooks a partially harvested field, small flower gardens, and a quartet of black men and boys loading bushels of produce onto a two-horse truck.

Other paintings share walls with shelves of rough lumber. A dozen soft-covered journals lie stacked on a lower shelf, their curled pages filled with hand-written accounts of events that have happened and events that have yet to happen.

Lina the Gnome has lived in this house for perhaps two, maybe three, centuries. Time for her is vague, chronology meaningless. Some suppose she is the energy, the source and soul of what has become the neighborhood, but she is certain that she is merely a component of fate.

It is she, not a child, in that upstairs window.

A Capella

Hot and humid, and rat bastard politicians. Not that Charlie Fish's father and his crew had nothing to do with the projects. Six buildings, fourteen stories of brick and shadow that dim the streets where *Golden Guineas* protect what's left of the neighborhood from *Young Satans*.

Baseball bats and gloves clutter the four steps of stoop in the schoolyard behind Christ the King Church and School. Three girls sit there, listening to voices *a capella* from seventeen-year-old tough guys with T-shirts, dungarees and cigarettes.

They are under the stoop in what they call the echo chamber, at a door to the school's basement. They're snapping their fingers, tapping their feet, and struggling through a song new to them.

Cogootz, top tenor with a sweet and soaring falsetto, knows all the harmonies, all the words. Annoyed, he says: "Fish, no. Into the bridge, we go up, you go down. Start it off again, man, let's get it this time."

Charlie Fish is the bass. He's tall, tough and wacky. One of the girls on the stoop, the one with the ankle bracelet, is his.

Mike, quiet kid, not as slim as the others, wavy black hair, is second tenor.

Vinny Blond is short and he's baritone and wears an

emblem off a Ford V-8 where the buckle of his garrison belt used to be.

The four sing and grin because now they're getting it, now close harmony bounces around the concrete walls of the echo chamber, out to the schoolyard, and into the streets, alleys and backyards of the neighborhood.

The girl with the ankle bracelet suddenly stands and leans over a rail at the top of the stoop. "Charlie," she calls down. "*Satans.*"

Harmony stops, the girls head out, don't look back.

At the schoolyard gate, four faces hard and dramatic. Diddybopper haircuts greased and glossy. Bargain store pants pegged tight at the ankles, narrow belts, and white t-shirts. One wears a shiny, red vest.

The *Guineas* scramble for the baseball bats. Charlie Fish, his bat shouldered like *Alley Oop*, his big voice: "What you want here? Get fucking lost."

The *Satan* with the red vest twists, right hand to left hip, comes back with a zip gun. The crack of a bullet and the smell of gunpowder. No hits, a sloppy run. A *Satan* falls, gets up, falls again under the slams of DiMaggio wood.

A woman screams.

Red Vest beats it around a corner, into a building, and the *Guineas* stampede him to the roof. He makes it to the edge, turns, spreads his arms in surrender, and wails the sound of fear.

Charlie Fish shuffles, swings at a high and outside, and a noise from the *Satan's* throat scratches the hot and humid. He tumbles into a blur that tries to fly, but bounces off a fire escape and lands like a rag on a neat line of ash cans.

A victory run, then a strut. Like the generations of neighborhood sentries before them, they had performed nobly. Now to the candy store, egg creams and pretzels. And shut up. Don't say nothing about nothing.

But Vinny Blond says something. He's excited and he's smoking, dragging deep. "You guys know what this is?"

"Yeah, yeah, we know," Charlie Fish says. "Schoolyard murder. When you gonna stop with that crap?"

"It ain't crap, man," Vinny says. "Lina ain't crap."

"So the neighborhood disappears now because a fucking monkey flies off a roof? It ain't the projects no more?"

"Yeah, well, we'll see."

"Fullashit. Lina too."

"Better stop with that shit, Fish," Cogootz says.

"Nobody's fullashit," Vinny Blond says. "Lina's here since before the neighborhood. You seen the picture, her and the dogs."

"Everybody seen it. So what?"

"So she's around too long to be an ordinary midget, and she can't be fullashit."

"Yeah?"

"Yeah."

"Tell her to look in those bullshit books she got, find out what number's coming out tomorrow."

"That ain't important."

"Vinny Blond, you're a dickhead," Charlie Fish says, looking to Cogootz, to Mike. "A real jerk-off, this guy. Money ain't important."

"Maybe he's right," Cogootz says.

"You too?"

"If it ain't right this time, there could be another guy gets whacked, different guy, you know? In the schoolyard, I mean."

"Just keep singing, Cogootz, and the neighborhood got nothing to worry about."

"Holy shit, Fish. My father says the same thing."

"Yeah, see?"

The Tailor

The neighborhood woke before dawn. Milk cans clanged, a rooster crowed, a dog barked. Shadows glided on tenement shades, while the stained-glass windows of Christ the King Church sent muted hues into the churchyard. Beyond the yard's brick wall, a cop clip-clopped his horse past dark storefronts.

The horse turned at the corner and stopped across from the church, where the man from Bari stood at his shanty stacking newspapers on crates, headlines readable in the thin glow of a kerosene lamp. The lamp, with tins of cigars and tobacco, candies and candles, sat on the pine panel that was his counter.

"Everything okay this morning, Tony?" the cop asked.

The *barese*'s name was not Tony; cops called Italians Tony.

"Everything good," the *barese* said, handing the cop a newspaper.

The cop saluted, made a sound with his throat, and his horse resumed its hollow rhythm.

The fruit and vegetables store and its sidewalk stand had been open all night. This was not unusual. The store's owner, a *calabrese*, with his face of leather, never slept more than a few hours at a time. He finished hosing his display of goods with water pirated from a johnny pump, shoved his cap to the back of his head, and sat with coffee to enjoy the last of the morning stars.

Where the cop left the block, slants of light seeped from between the planks of the stable's walls. The tailor, Enzo Burgundi, quick-stepped past the stable to the newsstand. He picked up a cigar and *Il Progresso*, wished the *barese* a good day, and saluted the *calabrese*.

He stepped across the sidewalk to his shop, where a four-foot statue of San Gennaro, dressed in wooden robes of gold, silver and reds, stood in the show window, next to a clothes dummy. The dummy wore a jacket of a fine black wool.

This wake-up happened every morning, and not the cop, not the *barese* nor the *calabrese* would report that, as the tailor keyed into the glass-paneled door of his shop, two brothers of the stable, Carlo The Arab, with the skin of an Arab, and Occhi, with eyes that looked away from each other, pushed in behind him.

Burgundi, a small timid man, resisted and surprised the thugs with pushing and kicking. But they overpowered him and jostled him to the door at the top of the cellar stairs.

"Give us what the Sardinian left and no harm will come to you," one of the stablemen said.

"No harm will come," the other said.

The tailor, stammering, but willing to give up what he had sworn to protect, moved to retrieve it. The Arab, the stronger of the two brothers, may have thought the tailor was resisting again, slammed his fist into his narrow chest and heaved him down the slant of wood stairs to the dirt of the cellar floor.

This floor spread underneath a stone wall and continued into the stable. They dragged the limp man through the door in that wall. Hens scrambled and horses shied, and not till they tried to stand him up did the brothers know that Carlo the Arab had killed Enzo the tailor.

From the dead man's pockets they took bills and coins, keys, and the cigar from the newsstand.

"Go find the purse," The Arab, short of breath, said. "And the letter. Don't forget to leave the letter."

"Give me the cigar," Occhi said.

"Just go," The Arab said, and kicked a spade into the stable ground.

Occhi climbed back up to the shop, careful to bolt the doors behind him. In the thinning darkness he locked the front door, rummaged through dozens of bolts of fabric on shelves and bins, stacks of unfinished garments on tables, and in boxes stocked with socks and collars and factory-made shirts. In the back room, he overturned the drawers of the desk that stood near the sink. He looked into the ice box and the bread box, and found no purse.

Back to the front of the shop, he took the letter, soiled and wrinkled, from his pocket and pinned it on the back of the clothes dummy's jacket.

Out the rear door, he let it snap-lock behind him. Scrambling down the iron steps and across the cinder-topped alley, he swore at the stupidity of his brother for slamming the tailor dead before finding the purse.

And only now, paces from the stable, did he realize that Don Cesare Strachi, whom the brothers had been trying to please by finding the purse, would accuse them of taking it and keeping it for their own profit. Angered further by this, and by the smell of the smoke of a fine tobacco, he snatched the ax from the woodpile, lifted it above his head, and charged into the stable. The Arab sneered, but backed off, and handed Occhi the tailor's cigar.

The Lovely Lucia

The elevated railroad cut sharp shadows onto the stones that paved 9th Avenue, where Lucia Burgundi stepped from a horse car and headed for the pier.

She had not been there since three years past, ferried from the confusion of Ellis Island. But the smells of the shushing river, the hot corn, frankfurter and pretzel wagons brought that morning to her.

There had been drizzle and fog and a kind of chill she'd never felt in Salerno. Enzo Burgundi, whom she'd come to *Nuovo York* to marry, emerged from the fog, a well-pressed figure bearing anticipation as uncertain as hers, but as refined and handsome as in the photo Papa had handed her nearly a year before.

"He is a tailor. Successful," Papa had said, his neopolitan tongue careful with this important talk. "He assures a good life and a home as fine as any in *L'America.*"

"*A zia* has done this, I think, Papa," Lucia said, smiling, as if uncovering a secret.

"Yes. She received his letter interested to know if she was yet a wife. Of course she is, and knowing him since childhood as honorable, she came to me for permission to name you to him. He has viewed your miniature and asks for approval to write to you."

How unexpectedly the first minutes of Enzo returned now, the way he had taken her under his umbrella, how she took his arm, as if they were not strangers. He smelled of flowers and, as in his letters, called her *Bella* and *Cara* and talked so much. He still talked so much, though not with her.

As an easy breeze from the river chilled Lucia, others jostled into positions to eye the passengers streaming through the ferry gate. She settled on the sunny end of a bench, prepared for as much patience it took for Rosina to be received, inspected and ferried from the island.

Rosina was younger than Lucia by two years, taller by inches, and prettier. But for her only sister, Lucia held no envy. And like Lucia, a focus of admiring glances, who had traveled unescorted *for* a man, Rosina traveled alone *from* a man.

She had written: *A good man chosen by Papa. As good perhaps as your Enzo, but one I could not love. And though you say that America is not without troubles, I cannot remain here, and where, without Mama, would I go but to you.*

By late afternoon Lucia had finished the bread and cheese she'd wrapped for herself and — *stupido* — in her bag, the jar of eggplant salad. In the excitement of this day, she'd forgotten to deliver it to the shop, to Enzo. But perhaps he would not anger at this special time. Perhaps he would show something of the care and kindness that ended in the hours after the wedding in the nearly empty Church of Christ the King.

Lucia pushed the hurt of that evening out of her mind and spent her thoughts on Rosina. Her hair, like Papa's, was black and thick and lustrous with curls as round as American dollars, while Lucia's black hair, like Mama's, fell thin and straight and only lustrous. It had always been their gray eyes and lips pouting as flowers about to open that revealed them as sisters.

With a commotion from the crowd, Lucia stood to see a scurry of people dragging valises, baskets and boxes down the ferry's ramp. Among them appeared Rosina.

Her face so bright, her hips in fashionable form, her spirited step, pleased Lucia. She seemed younger than her eighteen years, the same age Lucia had been when she'd walked that ramp with similar spirit.

Lucia called and waved and Rosina broke into a run, her satchel of patched canvas bouncing against her legs. Lucia ran too, and they collided and embraced, cried and laughed, and Lucia inscribed the moments into forever, for soon these exciting moments would fade. Soon Rosina would learn that Lucia's letters of happiness had been lies.

❊ ❊ ❊

Seated in a horse car, its floor strewn with straw that needed changing, and driven by an American who spit tobacco and cursed at his sad horses, Rosina must have seen bruises.

"Your Enzo, he beats you," she said.

Lucia looked to the street.

"For the wine?"

Lucia shook her head. "He needs no wine."

Rosina offered her hand, Lucia took it, and set it under her breast. "I am with his baby."

"And still he beats you?"

"He does not know."

"You must tell him."

"I do not want his baby."

"There is no choice, my sister."

"A child of Enzo's is certain to be a curse."

"You must not."

"There is the gnome."
"You must not."

* * *

The car rumbled into the din and excitement that was the neighborhood. Teamsters and cabbies whistling and shouting over the racket of horseshoes and iron rimmed wheels; men jockeying drays to nighttime quarters; men, women and children weaving this way and that, as if in a ritual, some toting stacks of piecework on their heads; a crippled man with a stock of suspenders hanging from an arm; a boy on a ladder lighting a street lamp.

"Here we are, then," Lucia said.

They helped each other from the car into air sweetened by a flash rain that had left puddles on the slate slabs of sidewalk. Men gazed as the sisters locked arms and stepped under awnings past storefronts crowded with sacks of beans and bushels of olives, salamis and salted meats hanging alongside bulks of cheeses, and shelves dusty with semolina from where the day's macaroni had been sold.

Rosina slowed at a window's display of lanterns, candles, pots and pans, and a machine that, according to Lucia, sang with the voices of Caruso and Patti.

The bell of a police wagon gonged in the distance.

Lucia hurried Rosina past a saloon with wafts of stale beer that wrinkled their noses. At an intersection tangled in noise and traffic, a bank's window advertised that inside one could manage money, send and receive letters, and secure a return across the Atlantic.

Where they turned the corner, a stout man stood writing in a small notebook while listening to a woman's battering dialect. The man's face, meaty and pocked, kind and worried, brightened as he looked to the sisters. He tipped his derby.

Looking over her shoulder, Rosina said: "He is Giuseppe Petrosino of your letters."

"From what I have written, you know?"

"He is *napulitan'*?"

"Yes, of *Padula*."

"He thinks fondly of you."

"He is a visitor to Enzo."

"Enzo has made Petrosino's coat?"

"His father is his tailor."

"He is not so short as you say."

"The derby lies for him," Lucia said, as if to approve. "And the look of Cuccio, you don't mention?"

Rosina smiled quickly. "Yes, yes."

They found the tailor shop dark and locked. Lucia knocked on the glass of the door, then peered through the show window beyond San Gennaro.

She called to a woman climbing the stoop next to the shop, a child asleep in her arms, his fingers tangled in her curls.

"Philomena, he is so beautiful, your Laurio. Like an angel he sleeps."

"Hello, Lucia. Yes, my angel." Philomena kissed the boy's head and looked to Rosina. "And your sister has arrived?"

"Yes, she has come."

"I am Philomena Matruzzo and wish you well."

"Thank you," Rosina said.

The church bell sounded seven times.

"Aha," Philomena said, her smile filled her wide face. Looking up to the simple bell tower across the street, she said: "Don Camillo tells us the hour and welcomes you."

"You have heard from the child's father?" Lucia asked.

"What do you think?"

"I think no."

"And still no letter, no money."

"You have seen Enzo?" Lucia asked.

"No," Philomena said, looking around as if she'd find him. "The door to your shop has been closed. The *barese* says that all the day customers have turned away."

Lucia looked to the newsstand, at an expectant look on the face of the *barese* as he leaned over his counter.

"We thought he went with you to greet your sister," he said, and to Rosina: "Hello, Signorina."

"Hello," Rosina said with a shy curtsy.

"He took his newspaper and cigar this morning, but I have not seen him since. No one has seen him."

"I will be upstairs, Lucia," Philomena said, pushing open the door to the building.

Lucia keyed open the shop, a bell above the door jingling lightly. She fired the kerosene lamp that sat on a worktable among patterns and cuts of fabric, picked up *Il Progresso* from the floor's black and white tiles, dropped it on the table, and returned to it for the date — *15 March, 1905; Wednesday.*

Moving the lamp to the counter in front of the shelves and bins, where bolts of material belonged, she found fabrics on the counter, others on the floor, with spilled boxes of collars, socks and garters. She skated her hand along the surfaces of the steam press. "It is too cold. No work has been done." She looked to the door. "The door was locked."

In the back room she found a drawer of Enzo's desk on top of the desk, another in the sink, one on top of the icebox.

"See here," Rosina called, pointing to a tear of paper pinned to the black jacket on the clothes dummy.

Lucia stepped to the scrap of paper, its edges torn and soiled, crude sketches of coffins and knives bordering the trace of a hand blackened with pencil.

You have more money than we have. We know of your wealth. If you do not like to be without a husband we want $500 that you are to enter into an envelope and put under the feet of the saint so we know you obey us. You will hear from us. We will know if you go to the police and you will no more see your husband.

A calculation so quick. "I must go to Petrosino," she said, and rushed to the street.

The Black Hand

Suddenly alone, Rosina sat, stood, sat again. The shop felt dark now, its shadows threatening, and when the bell above the door jingled it startled her. A child — no, a woman — in skirts of many colors, a bonnet the color of rust, a wave of black hair falling above amber eyes.

Rosina had watched — from a distance, because she'd been wary — Lucia and the other children run to greet the grinning gnomes perched like *fantoccini* atop a road show's donkey cart. This gnome, with a face that could have been a man's, allowed no distance. And, like the gnomes of the road show, she wore finger rings of coral, copper and silver, while larger rings dangled from her ears.

"Lucia is not here?" she asked, her voice that of a bold child.

Rosina held a breath. "She is soon to return." She moved the lamp to better see the gnome.

"I think the husband is not here." A corner of the gnome's mouth curled down, hardened her eyes and squared her chin.

"He is not here," Rosina said.

The gnome's face softened. "I am Lina. Do you know of me?"

"I have heard."

"You are the sister, then."

A careful smile broadened the gnome's face, making

delicate its husky features. From her skirt she took a small paper sack and, with the moves of a tin toy, set it on the worktable.

"For Lucia," she said, opening the door to the street and holding it. "It means nothing. Her baby will be healthy and cause much notice to Lucia."

As she left, her skirts lifted a whirl of dust from the door's threshold, then settled before Lucia returned with Joe Petrosino, Detective Sergeant, boss of the Italian Squad.

His coat hanging open in the warm evening, he lifted his derby, smiled shyly and said: "This young lady is Rosina?" Then let the hat drop back on his baldness.

"Yes, my good sister welcomed with this trouble. No one would blame her should she leave."

"I would not leave — "

"I am sorry for this trouble," Joe said, bowing slightly, as Lucia pointed to the letter pinned to a shoulder of the wool jacket.

Leaving it in place, Joe read it, removed it, read it again.

"They will kill him because I have come to you, Giuseppe?"

"No one can say, Signora," he said, shaking his head slowly, avoiding Lucia's eyes. "But there is no mistake in coming to me."

Joe's words had always been few, and these few stunned her, as if he knew and approved of what she had calculated so quickly, *We will know if you go to the police* — and become free of Enzo.

She held her breath, forced herself to see Petrosino's black eyes for a suspicion, an accusation, a recognition of guilt. But he calmly took his notepad from an inside pocket and folded the Black Hand letter into it. He motioned to *Il Progresso* on the table.

"The newspaper he buys in the mornings?"

"Yes. It was there." Lucia pointed to the floor, her voice pitched. "The gas has not been lit; the smell of cigar is of last night. The drawers of the desk in the back are overturned." She motioned to scatters of materials on the counter and on the floor, to upturned shirt boxes. "Garments have been disturbed and the fabrics too."

"Was there anything of exceptional value?" Joe asked.

"Silks and taffetas of high quality," Lucia said, shuffling through fabrics that had been tossed. "But they are still here."

"The door was locked when you arrived?"

"Yes."

"I think there is a rear door," Joe said, stepping into the upset of the back room, and finding the door to the back alley locked. He turned to the cellar door, slid open its bolt, and asked for the lantern. Climbing down the dark stairs, he called: "The door to the stable, it is always bolted?"

"Yes," Lucia said. "It is locked now?"

"Yes, from both sides."

Joe climbed back up. "You have been offered arrangements of protection?"

"Yes. Two men spoke with Enzo. He said he would speak with you."

"They were here, when?"

"Three or four weeks. Enzo said they were polite and spoke badly of the Black Hand. He did not speak with you?"

"No. And for weekly amounts they would guard you from danger?"

"Yes."

"Did you see them?"

"No."

"And he refused them?"

"It is difficult for Enzo to part with money."

❋ ❋ ❋

For a few more dollars a month Enzo Burgundi could have done the right thing. A nickel ride on the "L" or a trolley to an apartment with steam heat, a bathroom, electricity, a telephone.

Instead he and Lucia lived on the second floor of a five-story tenement with damp, dark stairways, an unheated toilet on each landing shared by four flats, each with rooms hooked together like box cars. Eleven dollars a month (he spent nearly as much on the cigars) for 325 square feet of kitchen, front room and bedroom. Airless and hot in summer, its walls sweated dampness that in winter steamed with the heat of the coal stove.

Lucia spent hours in that kitchen. Cooking, washing dishes and clothes, wiping coal dust from walls, sweeping and scrubbing bare wood floors on hands and knees before the relief of Mass on Sundays.

During morning hours, when a narrow angle of sun brightened the kitchen, she'd spent peaceful moments at the window tending her pots of mint, basil and oregano, or gazing out at mothers with babies and children shouting and laughing with street games. But only after having lived there for three years, and on a morning during the January last, did she learn of the hollow under the windowsill.

Awakened, but still in bed that morning, she'd heard Enzo moving about. He had not berated her in some days, had not forced himself upon her, and she would not break the peace if she quickly prepared his breakfast.

Setting her feet on the cold floor, she held closed her night-dress and, seeing into the kitchen, her pots of herbs had been moved from the window to the table's porcelain top. The windowsill had been removed also, and Enzo, still in his night clothes, reached into the exposed hollow, took from it a cracker tin and dropped something into it.

As he replaced the sill and the herbs, Lucia returned to bed and waited for him to demand breakfast. This he did not angrily, though neither he nor she spoke as he dressed, drank the coffee she poured, and ate toasted slabs of bread she'd sprinkled with olive oil and sugar.

She helped him with his coat and hat, and he responded with a closed-mouth grunt. She held open the door as he stepped into the building's hall, closed and locked it behind him, and stayed at the window till he walked from her view.

Quickly, quietly, as if someone were to hear, she removed the potted herbs from the window, and a vague significance of the old penny she'd picked up from the sidewalk some days before came to mind.

She jiggled away the sill, bared the hollow. Cold from it chilled her. She reached in, removed the cracker tin and, from it, plucked a brown envelope that held a fold of dollars many times the amount Enzo had refused her for Christmas.

The hurt twisted her mouth. "Not a tree, not a table cloth, not a sweet word."

Her gift had been some few yards of material from the shop. A canceled order, but a sturdy wool of tan and green plaid — at forty cents a yard, Enzo noted — that did not become her. But it was warm and needed no lining, and from it she fashioned herself a coat, cutting it to fit loosely, though she'd not yet known of a baby.

"Not a candle, not a glass of wine. Stingy bastard. Not a card." Then tears, and a return of the bitterness that had soured her breath and renewed itself as when she'd set eyes on the knives and coffins of the Black Hand letter.

※ ※ ※

She lowered the shop's lamps and looked to the street, still and silent, no moon, no stars, shadows like folds of wool. She let go a sigh and took the old penny from a dusty corner of her bag. "This I return to you," she whispered, and placed it at Gennaro's feet.

She looked to Rosina. Worn by three weeks of ship's travel and by the trouble of this day, she'd dropped into slumber, her head in her arms on the work table. Lucia wiped dribble from the sleeping sister's lips, then sat, comforted by sounds of childhood sleep.

Until Lucia left, they slept in a corner room, under a window filled with the smells of the farm, while the Mastiff, Cuccio, with eyes of a jealous lover for all but the sisters, slept at the door.

It had been a DiStasi daughter — 'a zia to the young sisters — a patient tutor who taught them the culture and ancient language that flourished in her *core napulitan'*; the respected *zia*, who had tutored in her students a similar heart.

Mathematics came easy to Lucia, but the younger Rosina had been the better student, eager for literature and history, and for one aged book that moved her to sketching its woodcuts of saints and angels.

She had overheard '*a zia* joke of a DiStasi cousin with five children, blessed with catching the seeds of conception by simply holding the hand of a man; and Rosina, impressive at fourteen years, held only the sleeve of any boy with enough nerve to ask her to dance.

Lucia watched this precious sister lift her head quickly, awakened perhaps by the rattle of the Bowery's elevated train, just blocks away.

"Sister, you are certainly a widow?" she asked.

Lucia turned and stepped to where fabrics still lay strewn on the floor. She gathered the finest of them, placed them on the counter, then let a length of black taffeta unfurl before her.

"This would make an attractive dress for a widow."

"What of the baby?"

Lucia darted her eyes into the eyes of her sister. "The gnome visited here, I think."

"Yes," Rosina admitted.

"And she left something?"

Rosina stood, stepped around the table, folded her arms. "You must not have what she left."

"It would be difficult to love a child of Enzo's."

"Together we will love it," Rosina said.

Looking to where the knife letter had been pinned, Lucia clasped Rosina's hands in hers and held them to her heart. "Then you will help me love it."

Bulldog Joe

His detectives called him *Bulldog Joe*. They bragged that he spoke the dialects of the *Mezzogiorno* — Naples, Calabria, Sicily; knew Latin of the Church and librettos of Italian opera. He charmed cooperation from good guys, muscled it from bad guys, dazzled the press, and went to Mass nearly every morning.

Built like a johnny pump, his neck was a no-neck, his shoulders heaps of muscle, his legs sturdy and short. Too short. Remarks, usually in a brogue, boomed that when the chubby dago got his vertical measured for the job, he must have been standing on three or four inches of greenbacks.

That's the way things were in 1883, the year a bridge connected the City of New York with the City of Brooklyn. Since then, the Brooklyn County of Kings and three other counties got pulled into the city, and the city promoted its shortest cop from Patrolman to Detective Sergeant and boss of the small, six-man Italian Squad. Black Hand cases, knife letters, kidnaps, bombs and murders.

Bulldog Joe found it necessary, the Squad liked to say at the bottom of a bottle of wine or a pitcher of beer, to kick Black Hand ass and let people watch him do it. And people watched when he'd caught a gander at a Black Hander, an oil can suited in a well tailored rig, a foot on a shoeshine box, a dirty kid slapping a rag on a boot that didn't need shining.

Joe's Squad had collared the guy months before — he'd firebombed a drug store and beat the druggist who ignored a Black Hand letter, and Joe walked him from a fancy whore house to a station house — in no rush, to give reporters time to show up, kicking him in the ass once in a while. But the worst thing that happened to the guy was that he beat the arson charge and Joe needed to square that.

The guy flipped the shoeshine kid a coin, flashed a pinky ring, and hoofed down the street. He must have felt eyes on him. He turned and caught Joe trying to look like sidewalk and, feeling a frisk coming, he sprinted, dumped a gun in the gutter and scrambled through a knot of mothers and grandmothers into a butcher shop.

Joe caught up with him in the walk-in box, cornered where a side of beef hung from a ceiling hook. The bomb thrower had about half a head on Joe, and being trapped must have got him balls. He pushed out of the corner and fired up a fist that Joe saw coming, got under it, let go a right that found the guy's face, and a left that found more face.

The guy took the clobbers till Joe tossed the beef into a sway, yanked the guy into its come-back, and watched him crumble, his face filled with stupid.

Out on the sidewalk, Joe finished up with a half dozen slaps and slams. Then he cuffed him, held a pose like Kid McCoy and called to the street: "You see how tough is the Black Hand? See these fine clothes and rings of gold that you have paid for, this filth you are afraid of?"

"You got nothing, Petrosino," the oil can said.

"I got you, *scifoso*."

"The gun is gone."

"There are others."

"You'll put on me."

"And what do you think?"

The Italian newspapers hammered Joe, complained that he knocked out more teeth than a dentist, but the American papers loved him, praised *The Detective in the Derby,* and admitted that Little Italy needed his kind of push-around. It was why victims, usually afraid to talk to cops, felt easy talking with him.

❀ ❀ ❀

The neighborhood still nighttime quiet, Joe stood on the steps of Christ the King Church, listening for a sign, a whisper from the street. The dim light of the tailor shop should have told him something, or San Gennaro, or the dummy with the black jacket. But no.

Joe had sometimes sat in that shop with Enzo and a pot of coffee, while Enzo hemmed and measured and cut, and went on about the collusions of Verdi and Garibaldi; on and on about connected hits on President McKinley and King Umberto. But with all the chatter, the tailor never squawked on the two suited gorillas who gabbed bad on the Black Hand and pitched protection.

Joe stepped into the candlelight of the church. With smells of recently burned incense pleasing him, he sat, still listening for a name, a face, a direction. But he heard only the voice in his mind — Lucia Burgundi's voice, and the sadness in her gray eyes, the promise in her pouting lips, and the sway of her skirts as she stepped from the rear of the shop with a plate for her husband. She'd whacked him silly that day, kicked him under the heart with warm and cold thunder, a delight he would have held had it not come from the wife of an honorable man.

He'd kept it buried, but when she'd run to him earlier, pulled him to where he could see tears behind her eyes — *Giuseppe, come please … Enzo … knife letter* — she nudged the thunder. She led him into the shop, to the Black Hand letter, and he read what was not written: the kidnappers seeing Lucia ignore the warning about going to the police, and that the beautiful wife would be a beautiful widow, alone and vulnerable to the fears and temptations certain to find her.

As if he heard the message he'd been waiting for, he took the pad still in his inside pocket, turned to his notes. *Enzo shop. Robbery? Kidnaping, ransom. No visible break. The shop searched, the tailor taken. Back door snap locked. Street door locked. From inside? Outside? Cellar, dark — bolt secure on the door to the stable …*

… And the stable's tales of torture and murder, informants giving up stutters and shakes and nothing else. Now he'd see what Benny Bats could give up.

Benny Bats

Benito Carlucco. A smooth talker in English or in *napulitan'*, quick with a buck, a charmer. An all-alone bookmaker who never ducked a payoff. A good fellow for the kids who chased him for coins and for cripples who could not.

Hair like patent leather, he dressed swell and flashed a set of choppers under a Puccini kind of moustache. Pushing five-eight, he was a giant for a *napultan'*. Even with the two or three inches of scar that rimmed his left jaw — and maybe because of it — uptown dames with rich daddies, and neighborhood janes with rouged lips and shaded eyes kept watch for Benny, and Benny kept eyes for what could hurt him and what could help him.

A loner since the blizzard of '88 dropped fifty inches of snow on his father — dead from a heart no one knew was bad, ten-year-old Benny grew up fast.

No one had seen Papa in the whiteout, or heard him in the wind that blasted through the alley to the vacant lot. Then the thaw ... and Mama's face screwed tight, screaming and growling that her coward of a husband had gone to hell and left her with the problem of Benito ... and beating the boy's ass and legs with Papa's strap because he had not gone to hell, too.

But the ten-year-old did the right thing for his father by

doing the right thing for his mother. Summer, winter, Monday to Saturday, Benny got to the market before the sun, stocked the cart with fruits and vegetables, and set up on the corner that the old man had been working with a weekly shake to a crew of siggies — Sicilians — the brothers and half brothers of Clutch Hand Joe Morello, a bad man with a hand locked into a claw.

These guys did counterfeit, gambling and loansharking. They stole and sold horses, ran bogus Italian lottery tickets, wrote Black Hand extortion letters, and packed revolvers. They ate from the top, but paid tribute to cutthroats in Sicily.

Years on that corner, right up to Benny's eighteenth birthday, profits going up and down, the shake going up and up, a Morello collector — a guy with the face of a mule and crust under manicured fingernails — bit into a plum, made a face and spit the mouthful into a bushel of cherries.

A burn seeped into Benny's gut and aced to his head. He went for a paper bag under the peaches, hurled it, and the wrench in the bag caught the guy on the side of the head, making a dent and a trickle of blood.

The guy shook off the dizzy and fixed his hat. But two guys with bats caught up to Benny, shoved him into an alley, beat him into a seizure he'd never had before. Shaking on the concrete floor, his brain lost in some kind of black, the batters disappeared up Bowery, their legs dangling like play time from the tailgate of a rag picker's truck.

In a few days he limped out of New York Hospital, ribs and hips in the pains, but he checked his pearly whites a few times and each time they numbered thirty-two. The only re-arrangement his face took were the stitches on his jaw. But he was still pretty, still spiteful, and limped when it rained or when he wanted to.

With all the transactions in his head and in his pockets,

he took action — policy and sports — all on his own, and built the book to four, six dollars a week, then fifteen or twenty. All he had to do was keep a glance for Louisville sluggers and guys like Joe Petrosino.

But on a sunny afternoon, about a year before the tailor got grabbed, Joe jumped him. Benny was quick on his feet, and had he seen it coming, would have bolted into a wind. But Joe muscled him into a hallway on Houston Street and found pockets of his double sawbuck suit stashed with a poke of greenbacks and stacks of Italian lottery tickets.

"They're honest-to-God legit, Petrosino."

"Made in a cellar."

The lottery swindle worked before it got old and pigeons got scarce. Still, for renegade Benny it was pudding, and up the giggy to the Brooklyn Camorra clan that had been running the gyp for years.

"What happened with the fruit wagon?" Joe asked.

"They took it."

"Morello."

"Yeah."

Joe fanned the greenbacks. "Where'd this come from?"

"You know where it came from. I gotta do something. My mother gotta eat."

"You got a felony here with these tickets."

"It ain't a felony, Petrosino."

"A felony. But if I lose a few, it's a misdemeanor."

"Yeah, so?"

"Let's see how we get along."

"What about the cash?"

"Let's see how we get along."

Joe booked Benny on the misdemeanor, talked a man-to-man on the way to Police Court, got him low bail, and started pinching Morello joints and runners till the siggies got the message that, as long as they left Benny Bats to his small book, Joe left their spots alone.

That was how Joe did the right thing for Benny, and that was why Benny did things for Joe — like living in the dingy room above a grocery store that wholesaled olive oil. If he reached out the window near his bed he could have touched the sign — *Rice, Dried Vegetables, Tinned Foods, Macaroni, Olive Oil*.

He picked his jacket off the bed and walked down the back stairs to the grocery's kitchen. The grocer's wife wiped her hands on her apron and flashed Bennie the smile that made dimples.

The woman carried the kind of chubby Benny went for, her face pretty when her hair wasn't falling over it, like when she was lying down.

"Anything?" Benny asked.

"He tells me nothing." She made a face, threw up a hand.

"Anybody talking about a painting?"

She shrugged, held it. "What painting?"

"Never mind."

"I'm making the olive salad." She made dimples again. "You want?"

"Deliver it."

"When?"

"Late. Knock on the door."

❋ ❋ ❋

On the street Benny found the usual noise and horseshit-dust floating in the late slants of sun. On the corner, under the red and yellow umbrella of his peanut wagon, Georgie Nuts Pugliesi looked like a Macy's Santa Claus. Short and round and red-faced, a gray scarf hanging from a pocket of the brown corduroy jacket that he'd worn since crossing the Atlantic years back, he handed a bag of peanuts to a junkman, his horse annoyed with the smoke and whistles of the roaster.

"Hey," Benny said.

"Hey, Benny Bats. You look sharp."

"I always look sharp." Benny took a bag of peanuts off the top of the roaster.

"Put those back, take the others. Hot."

"Getting too warm to sell these things?"

"No, this weather's good. I gotta stay here anyway. I leave, I lose the spot. You know how it is."

"Who you see for this corner now?"

"Some guy, supposed to be with the Sicilians. Mafia, he says. Who knows? For a dollar a week, nobody bothers me and I don't ask. When you gonna let me work with you?"

"Siggies hear you're with me, we both catch a beating."

"Ain't what I hear."

"What's that?"

"A truce with Strachi," Georgie said.

"You hear that, huh?"

"And you're on your way up."

"How do you hear what I don't hear?"

"Can't be you don't hear, Benny."

Benny grinned. He'd heard. "I gotta go."

The roaster whistled.

"Wait, Benny. I'm looking to get an okay up the Central Park, get some roasters up there. Maybe the Bronx Zoo. Maybe you'll get to know somebody."

"That's the city."

"Yeah, so? Still you need somebody."

"What about the siggie who takes your dollar?"

"They're all horseshit, these cowboys."

"Give me time. Things are happening."

"I thought you didn't know."

"Yeah, but let me go see what I don't know."

Georgie tossed Benny another bag of nuts. Benny snatched it and hoofed a block out of his way to skirt a Morello joint on Prince Street. At Elizabeth Street he quick-turned into an alley that took him to the door of *La Stella di Napuli*.

The place looked the same as what Petrosino had told him. Planks spanning three beat up barrels made the bar. Working guys, their shovels and picks in a corner, stood gabbing and pouring red from bottles without labels.

On a rough plastered wall across from the bar a faded print of the *Madonna* hovering over the Bay of Naples looked down at a table topped with linoleum and at men playing cards without eights, nines and tens.

Sawdust on the floor, fresh and acidic, tickled Benny's nose. He stepped to an alcove near the kitchen, where The Ox sat at a table with a steak and the bottom of a bottle of red, this one with a label. He wore a pampered moustache, a head of dense black hair, a keg of a chest.

The table was round, draped by a cloth of coarse linen. The Ox wore a *mappin'* of the same linen, corners of it tucked under a stand-up collar.

He looked up at Benny, motioned with a fork to a chair. "Sit."

"How the hell did you find this place?" Benny asked.

"I told you it was a dump," The Ox said, his dialect from the streets of downtown *napuli*, his tongue loose with the bottle at his elbow. "But the food's good."

"I almost didn't find it. Why here?"

"The building is his, keeps a *cumare* up the stairs." The Ox picked up the bottle by its neck and showed it to somebody behind Benny. "Forty-five years old, he wants to be twenty. And he's asking about the tailor's wife, wants to know who's out after her."

"The husband isn't even cold yet," Benny said.

A blast of heat and a skinny kid with an apron as long as his legs came out of the kitchen. He delivered a bottle, opened it and walked off.

The Ox forked the steak, lifted it, showed off two inches of medium rare. "You want?"

"Steak. No more macaroni?"

"You want, yes or no?"

"No. What's up over here?"

"Something for you."

"Yeah, you said."

The Ox sat back and shrugged. "I said?"

"Yeah."

"I talk too much."

"I say nothing about what you talk," Benny said.

"Yeah, I think so. Don Strachi trusts you. Still I must keep my tongue quiet."

"Keep it quiet, or let it talk, makes no difference to me. But why does he trust me? There must be others he trusts."

"He is not done distrusting them yet."

"And me?"

"You're an earner, he says. A victory over his enemies."

"Morello? The Sicilians?"

The Ox nodded. "He will protect you from them and you will be grateful and loyal out of fear of losing Camorra protection."

The Ox went back to his steak, cut a triangle and forked

it. "There is talk of the painting?" He stuck the triangle in his mouth.

"Nobody knows about a painting. Nothing. I don't either."

The Ox rubbed a thumb against bunched fingertips. "Gone. Lost."

"From where?"

The Ox shook his head. "A priest had it. A Sardinian. He was with the tailor, so maybe the tailor knew something."

"Did he?"

"Nobody knows." The Ox shrugged

Benny sipped wine. "Don Strachi is late?"

"Over there." The Ox pointed with his chin.

Benny twisted to see Don Cesare Strachi at the door, puffed and smiling like enter-stage-right. Light gray suit as fine as any in Benny's closet, straw porkpie hat in his hand, bright white shirt and collar. Maybe forty, maybe forty-five, black cone eyes, nose square, scarred and broken; skin the color of roasted pork, close cut red hair on a head like a melon.

Even with the melon head, the comical space in his front teeth, he looked good for the up and coming camorrista Joe and the Squad had made him for, with histories as an earner, enforcer and loyal soldier — reports that went from The Ox to Benny to Joe Petrosino.

Taking the fall on a kidnap he didn't do, Strachi got fifty-four months. Then, part of the deal: *The siggies are strong in New York. Make a run up their backs. Construction, unions. Make respect.*

The right money got spent on the right people, court orders got hidden, and Strachi got sprung to New York with a wad of American cash and a passport.

Benny began to stand.

"Sit, sit," the Camorrista said, his voice wind and sand. He sat, picked up his glass, saluted The Ox and Benny, looked back to The Ox. "What, you don't shave?"

"The barbers. You closed them on Mondays."

"You have no razor?"

The Ox shrugged, looked ashamed. "I'll go now."

"Never mind now." Strachi motioned to the empty bottle. "You drank that?"

The Ox shrugged.

"Drink, and the tongue takes over the mouth," Strachi said and faced Benny. "So Benito is here."

"You call for me, I come, Don Strachi."

Strachi set his palms flat on the tablecloth, and in the usual mix of *napulitan'* and English, said: "Men like you — like us" — he motioned to include The Ox — "we earn, there is greed and jealousy, and fear that we cut into Morello interests. So we must sit again with them in that pigsty they call a restaurant, and accept the swill they call food. You have been there?"

"No," Benny said.

"So it is true what they say, that they have nothing to do with you."

"Not since they gave me a beating."

"A year now. They suspect that you are in the protection of the police. Morello is jealous for percentages that should be his."

Benny started to speak, Strachi cut him short.

"I have told him that you are with me." Strachi nodded, satisfied with the maneuver. "And with me you are protected from his bandits."

"I thought I was already with you."

"Yes, the olive oil. But you are valuable elsewhere too." Strachi set his hand on Benny's hand. "Valuable, Benito, and loyal, very important for new business." He took back his hand.

"You well speak the languages of two countries. Men take quickly to you. Women also, I understand." He grinned and nodded. "And you share with no one."

"No one."

"You will now see to our books, our operations, and share with us. No. We will share with you. Earn with us and keep more than you now keep for yourself."

"You have much trust in me, Don Cesare."

"I make a generous offer, but you are uncertain."

Benny caught a flash of anger in Strachi's eyes.

"I am uncertain only of myself. My operation is small and my books are simple. Yours is big and I fear failure."

"With me there is no failure."

* * *

The Hotel Monterey, eleven floors of class and old glitter, sat on West Twenty-third, at the foot of the Tenderloin. Its restaurant took reservations from the same crowds that fed at Delmonico's, the Waldorf, Rector's, and other palaces where theater swells ate and drank with judges and commissioners, and where Tammany Hall shysters and bagmen hustled favors and envelopes.

Tourists, rounders and gentlemen poured in and out of the classy joint, putting down bets, picking up wins and chancing a gander at one or two of Broadway's Florodora Girls, or Sam Clemens, or maybe Bat Masterson, the lawman, gambler, sports writer, and occasional partner to Benny, and the reason — according to Benny and the wide eyes who didn't know better — for the Bats moniker.

Joe liked the Monterey, far enough up on the 9th Avenue "L" from the neighborhood to keep Benny's cooperation a secret.

With thick-soled shoes that grew him an inch or two, Joe hoofed among tourists and the lonely headed for the sparkle and flesh of the Tenderloin. He crossed Twenty-third through a knot of top hats and tuxes, furs and satins, shining black Hansoms that were cabs, and a half dozen Franklins, Packards and Buicks.

He spotted Benny's pearly grin looking out from the lobby and went in.

"Joe, not for nothing," Benny said, "but what's with that face? You need a woman or something."

"What you got for me?" Sometimes Joe didn't like Benny.

"Maybe you don't like women."

Joe's eyes went black. "I have no time for bullshit. What do you have for me?"

"Easy, Joe, I'm breaking balls. Nice rig, fits you good. Who's the tailor? Your father, your brother?"

"Never mind my father, my brother. How do you know so much?"

"I know what everybody knows. Let's go sit. And take that pot off your head, or everybody in the joint's gonna know who you are. Your picture in the paper all the time, and you ask how I know about your father, your brother. *Cazz'.*"

They sat at the bar. Mirrors, marble and mahogany, brass and crystal. Joe set his derby on a stool, skated a palm across the top of his head, as if it had hair.

"Let's try the French," Benny told the man behind the bar.

The barman set down glasses, poured lightly, stepped away.

"What you wanna know first?" Benny asked Joe.

"The oil."

"I tried the wife. She says she knows nothing. I believe her. Anything I get comes from The Ox, and he says he's stupid on the oil thing."

"The painting."

"The painting is a guy eating or something. Worth a few bucks, supposed to be a scheme for the communists. Sounds like bullshit, but that's the word. They thought the tailor had it, but it got lost."

"Like the tailor got lost."

"No. The tailor got lost like this." Benny made a gun with his fingers, dropped the hammer. "The stable next to the shop. Patarama. The father, a vicious bastard, and three sons. Junk dealers, horse thieves, blacksmiths. They sell rabbits, chickens, whatever. Horses, carriages, all that shit. They live in that fucking place, Joe. Swamp guineas eating and sleeping there."

Benny leaned forward, dropped his voice. "They're with nobody, they're with everybody. Siggies, Camorra. They're looking for the painting, supposed to be that a priest gave it to the tailor to hide and hold. And to make a score with Strachi, they go for it, then write the knife letter for themselves."

"They killed him, why?"

"Animals don't need a reason."

"This came from who?"

"The Ox, but Strachi was sitting right there when he's telling me this, not real interested."

"Where's Carmine Tonno with all of this?"

"Nobody sees Happy Carmine. But he's around, Strachi don't make moves without him."

"Like Black Handing the tailor?"

"Strachi had nothing to do with that. I told you, they were looking to make a score with him. Anyway, that ain't major. Every zip off the boat that wants a ring on a pinky pulls that Black Hand shit."

"So, what's Carmine do when he's not around Strachi?"

"Just looking like he's not around. The Ox says it looks like he's scheming all the time. Got ideas for himself. Whenever there's a sit-down with Morello, Carmine's right up their ass. I told you all this."

"How do they know about the stable brothers?"

"I don't know. Maybe from Gaga. Slow."

"That's Apollo," Joe said. "He's around, but Carlo and the one with the eyes, they're in the wind."

"So they must figure the whole story."

"Yeah, and what's that?"

"Strachi's thinking that maybe they got the painting, and maybe they don't, but he's looking to whack these two for bringing heat on him."

Benny sat back and sipped, holding the wine glass with his pinky angled like highfalutin. "Hey, Joe, the wife. I got a gander at her."

Benny, quick and arrogant and cocky. Good liar, good stool. Sometimes Joe liked him.

"Never mind the wife," Joe said.

"Hey, by the way, the marshal wants his gun back. Can you do that?"

"Who?"

"Masterson. The marshal, sheriff, whatever he is."

"A friend all of a sudden?" Joe asked.

"What about it, the gun?"

"Let him get a new gun."

"The cane too. They took his fucking cane, your guys."

"How does he connect you with me?"

"The night you took me for the tickets, he got locked up for beating a pigeon out of some gelt. You forgot? In the cell we got talking."

"What did you tell him?"

"Nothing. I talk to you more than I talk to anybody. He

uses me, I use him. Mostly he uses me. Not a friend. I got no friends."

"A swordsman like you, no friends?"

"Just you. Who else could I trust? Nobody gives *'i cazz'* about nobody. That's why this neighborhood is on its way out. But you, you got friends all over the place. All right, you got enemies too, but you got me to look out for you."

The bar began crowding up. Joe took his hat from the stool. "Why do you want to know about the tailor's wife?" he asked.

"A doll face."

"Your head is clear."

"If I got a clear head, then Strachi got a clear head too. He wants to know who she talks with, what men are chasing after her."

"He told you this?"

"The Ox did. And maybe she got the painting."

"Does she?"

"Who knows?"

"What else you got?"

"Maybe you want to see Lina."

"The neighborhood ending again?"

"Maybe. But The Ox took Strachi to see her."

"The farmhouse?"

"The Monkey House."

Lina in the Monkey House

———

From the second floor windows of her farmhouse, Lina had watched the farms and woods around her become streets with elevated railroads, trolley tracks and tenements. She watched people make homes in the tenements, saw them crowd the streets, watched them build a church.

They had known of her and others like her before coming to America. Healers of man and beast, of bodies and souls. Lina had counseled prostitutes off bromide, laudanum and alcohol. And though never with a baby in her belly (probably never been laid, according to Italian Squad romeos), her milk ended infection and chased off evil spirits. She comforted the phantoms who walked and wailed through the nighttime neighborhood; some of them, she'd told Joe, have escaped graves trapped under "the hooves of horses."

For Joe the hooves of horses meant those of the Patarama Stable. He believed in the graves and would have been glad to hear from the strolling spooks if they had anything to put in a search warrant that a judge would sign.

He understood, too, Lina's affection for the neighborhood and her sadness that it would destroy itself.

"You will fix that," Joe had said.

"I cannot."

"Then why do you speak to change what you call inevit-able?"

"To keep from despair."

"So fate is no longer inevitable?"

"We shall see."

"How many years do you have?" Joe asked.

"There are no years for me."

"You will not answer."

"I have answered."

Joe respected Lina and the fate that he'd stopped trying to understand. To keep her from troubling his mind, he'd visited her only when he had to solve a mystery, find a bad guy, make a case.

There had been no secret that she had taken a liking to Bulldog Joe, so much so that the guys in the Squad broke his balls with a Valentine card signed with her name.

Joe never mentioned it. Maybe it really came from her.

* * *

Joe called from his desk: "Charlie, what are you doing?"

Carlo Corrao, tallest man in the squad, blue eyes, brown hair combed back in waves, always in a bright white shirt and collar. The young girls on Mulberry Street around headquarters called him "Handsome Charlie" and giggled when they did.

He and Joe had worked tours together long before Joe picked him up for the Squad. They'd rolled around the streets fighting psychos and bad guys, busted down doors, watched operas, shared philosophies, meals, bottles of wine.

He stepped to Joe's desk, dropped a report on it.

"Let's go to the monkeys," Joe said.

Charlie wrinkled his nose.

"We'll be quick. New suit?"

"Used to be. The new one's in the closet standing by."

"New tie, then."

"Yeah."

Tall enough to see over the dome of Joe's derby, Charlie picked up his boss's step and the two walked through neighborhood noise and good-morning weather to the stoop on Baxter Street, where scents of simmering garlic and potted lilacs mingled with the used air of the Monkey House. Above the stoop and the storefront next to it, five stories of tenement windows, open even on days not dry and warm, moved with the figures of men and monkeys.

Men and boys on the stoop, waiting to rent or buy monkeys from any one of six or seven flats, made way as the detectives climbed into the building — Joe watching Charlie lock his breath from the smells — then down a rear flight of cobwebs and wood steps that groaned like pain under their feet.

Opening the apartment door before Joe knocked, Lina looked up. In her arms, wrapped in a baby blue blanket, a wide-eyed monkey was feeding at her breast.

"Well, *Signore* Detective Petrosino has come to Lina as a policeman, has come for his future, or because he loves Lina?" She made a fake grab for Joe's *pescediel'* and he twisted away with a breath trapped in his throat.

The monkey, annoyed, lost its meal.

"Oh, so sorry little *pupata*," Lina said, and helped him retrieve it. "He was near death, this poor thing. The *putan'* that is his mother refuses him, and his *padron'* comes to Lina for the milk that brings him life."

Behind Lina, under a window that looked out on a glass-covered garden of early tomato and pepper plants, half a dozen young monkeys bunched in the corner of a cage, curious

with the visit. Two others, gray and bright eyed and not interested in the visitors, hunched on a table groping into battered
pots and filling their mouths.

"What is it they eat?" Charlie asked.

"Milk and bread," Lina said. "Stale bread the baker gives
me. And they are grateful."

Lina stepped back to see the tall Corrao. "Your name I
don't remember."

"Corrao."

"Yes, Beautiful Charlie."

"Handsome."

"Handsome Charlie, yes. Serious like Joe."

Gold hoops swung from Lena's ears as she exaggerated
a curtsy that bunched her skirts on the floor's linoleum. Still
with the monkey, she closed the door. Inside smelled better
than outside.

Joe played with thinking that if monkeys talked, they'd
sound like Lina. "*Piccerella*, put away the monkey," he said.
"Please."

Lina's face went sad, connected her eyebrows. "Petrosino
has no heart for you, motherless beast."

"Doesn't he hurt you?" Corrao asked.

"No more than any child." She put the monkey in a cage
and covered the cage with a cut of a horse blanket. She examined her tit and put it away. "Please sit so I don't look up."

They sat, Lina exaggerating a look of importance. "You
have come to Lina because Don Strachi has come to Lina."

"Why has he come?" Joe asked.

"For the light, the protection."

"Protection from what?"

"From others like him. And from Joe Petrosino" — Lina
flicked a ringed finger at Joe — "whose name they cannot say
without spitting."

"Who spits?"

"I don't see, I only know."

"Strachi talks of me?"

"Only for protecting him from your police. But I only pretend. There is no light for *male vita*."

"That is not all he wanted."

"He thinks the widow of the tailor knows of a painting."

"He said that?"

"I say that. But she knows nothing of it."

"You have talked with her?"

"No."

"She is surely a widow?"

"You know she is."

"Does she know?"

"She is eager to wear black."

"Where is the painting?"

"It is dark, I cannot see."

"What is it?" Joe asked. "From where does it come?"

"I cannot see it, so I don't know."

"And your books say nothing?"

"It is not important enough for the books."

"What else has he asked?"

"To know who killed the tailor."

"Who did?"

"You already know."

"But what do you know?"

"I see no faces."

"You told him that?"

"I did not tell him that I know they did it to please him."

"With the painting?"

"Yes, but he never will see it. It is less valuable to him than the charms of the widow."

"And she?"

"Hunger drives the wolf from the forest."

"She is hungry?"

"She believes she is."

"Where is the tailor?"

"Under dirt that is trampled by the feet of a horse."

Joe smiled quickly. "But is it not too dark for you to see under the dirt?"

"You find fun in what I say."

Lina seemed hurt; Joe let go the smile. "No, no, *Piccerella*."

"The stable ground holds many bodies," she said. "I don't see them, but I know what many know."

"There is torture?"

"For those who ignore the Black Hand letters." Her face became rigid. "You must know this."

"And the writers?"

"There are many writers."

"Like the men of the stable?"

"Yes."

"*Piccerella*, why didn't you come to me with what you know?"

"I have told you of the phantoms, but you turned your face."

"You have told me more now."

"You are listening now. And there is more on your mind, I think. The widow Lucia?"

Joe felt a blush. "It's not true that she is confused with sadness?"

"I have said she is eager to wear black. The face of the tailor was kind to most, but to her it was the mask of the goat." Lina lifted gentle eyes. "You show warmth for her."

Joe glanced at Corrao, Corrao looked to the monkeys.

"For all her charm," Lina said, "she is unhappy with believing that no one will have her. She is afraid of being alone, and worries that her sister will leave her. But Lucia needs more than the sister or you can give. For her sister, good sister, she is merely a burden that cannot be neglected. For you she is heart-ache."

"She is frightened."

"Her head is not clear, and for that she is frightened. She is not as unwise as you think, though not as wise as she thinks."

Joe stood, hands at his back.

"So, Petrosino, you have learned more of your heartaches than of Strachi."

Joe felt locked in Lina's gaze. "What else must I know of Strachi?"

"He fears you and vows to kill you."

"You will keep me safe."

"From those who would kill you. But the softness of your heart and the thickness of your head are the most dangerous."

The Camorrista
Visits Lucia

he rain had rinsed sidewalks, streets and gutters, and
left a breeze that stirred the smells of bread stores, bakeries
and the fish market into something almost pleasant. Lucia
wedged open the shop's door to let freshness help soothe the
upset the baby in her belly had been kicking up.

Pleasant to her, as if she'd not heard them before, were
the yelps of a clothesline pulley, the softened clangs of a distant
trolley, and the chatter of mothers and grandmothers bar-
gaining at sidewalk pushcarts.

But then came the fractured rhythms of a street organ.
My Merry Oldsmobile scraped at her ears and the man crank-
ing it annoyed her. She didn't like his monkey either, with those
fingers of a spider. She hurried to the cash register, snatched
a penny, and dropped it in the monkey's tin cup. "Now go someplace else, little beast. Please."

She explained to Rosina what a son-of-a-whore the song, the
organ, the man and the monkey were. And what an Oldsmobile
was and that it too was a son-of-a-whore. The both of them
laughing, Lucia scooped sleeves and collars from her sewing
machine and set them in front of Rosina at the pattern table.

Lucia returned to sewing, the machine's treadle squealing
under her feet. Because the door was open, the bell had not

jingled, and when this man entered the shop, his sudden presence startled her. She stopped sewing.

His face was gruff and unattractive, but his smile was not, even with the black rectangle between its two front teeth. Built stoutly, with the head of a *zuccon'* — a pumpkin — topped by a fedora, an overcoat draped his shoulders as if it were a cloak of aristocracy.

"Good day," he said, taking off the hat.

"Good day," Lucia said, sitting back from her work.

"Perhaps a little oil." His voice was soft and broken, his *napulitan'* not as fine as hers.

"Oil?"

"For the machine." He pointed his chin to the treadle.

A shorter man with a broad face stepped in quietly, a cone of white roses in his square hands.

"Oil, yes, I'll find some," Lucia said, nearly smiling.

"You are the Signora Burgundi?"

"Yes."

He bowed slightly, turned toward Rosina, bowed again, and took the flowers from the other man.

"I am Cesare Strachi, to pay respects."

Lucia stood, her eyes on the man. "Thank you, but we do not know that paying respects are yet in order."

"Excuse my clumsy words."

Lucia took the roses, smelled them, and found it was his cologne that had been pleasing her.

"They are beautiful," she said and set them on the pattern table as Rosina made room for them. "Please sit."

"There is business, but perhaps it is not a good time?"

"Please sit." Lucia kept her smile polite, curious, cautious. She sat again, her back now to the sewing machine.

Strachi moved quickly and smoothly for a man older than

Enzo, who'd been ten years older than Lucia. He settled at the edge of a chair, the fedora on his lap.

"Perhaps you have learned that I soon will own this building."

A rush of nausea. A thorn in her breast. She dropped her smile, flattened her eyes. "You will raise our rent. We have but a small business. There is barely enough." She held open her hands as if to show nothing.

"No, no, no, Signora. There is no raise to the rent." Strachi shook his head. His jowls jiggled, then stiffened with an amused smile as he looked to bins stocked with fabric, to the sewing machines, one of them new, and to a scatter of incomplete coats and jackets pinned with invoices.

"I regret I have concluded wrongly," Lucia said.

Strachi smiled. "I understand."

The ice man walked in, a block on his shoulder. The usually talkative man nodded uncertainly to Strachi, then walked to the rear room and loaded the ice box. As he left, kids scattered from his truck with stolen shards of ice.

In a few quiet moments the church bell gonged nine hours.

Lucia said: "But Giacalone has said that his children will someday own this building."

"Perhaps he has decided that they own other buildings. Be that as it may, I wish you to feel comfort with me. I intend to continue the same rental arrangements, and if that should prove troubling in this bad time, we will agree on others."

Lucia found it difficult to look into the slits of daylight in the black of Strachi's eyes, but she did, and avoided the eyes of the man at the door, the one called The Ox, she came to realize, because she'd heard of these two.

"And now I will leave you to your work." Strachi stood. "May I have a card of business?"

"There are no cards, but Rosina will give you one of our work orders. It will do for a card."

Rosina slid a work order from under the weight of a pin magnet and handed it to the man at the door.

"Until next time," Strachi said, a brightness in his face that Lucia had not at first noticed.

When he left, The Ox stepped behind him folding the blank work order into a pocket.

Rosina's face went wide and she giggled nervously.

"Peculiar, no?"

Lucia put the back of a finger to her lips.

"*Mala vita*?" Rosina asked.

"Camorra."

Now Rosina held a finger to her lips.

"You smiled sweetly for the one who gave the roses."

"He is Cesare Strachi," Lucia said. "He wishes us well."

She stepped to the counter before the shelves of stock, reached for a vase and held it as Rosina arranged the roses in it.

"Twenty-four," Lucia said.

"There is no perfume," Rosina said.

"Their beauty needs no perfume."

The Man in the Barrel

Occhi sidled into *La Stella di Napuli*, a peacoat slung over a shoulder. He had on a black sweater worn thin at the elbows, and the stocking cap of a dockworker. He set a hand on a bottle of red at the bar and leaned forward.

"Do you know me?" he asked the barman.

"Never seen you before."

"A glass."

The barman put a water glass on the bar and filled it. Occhi sipped slowly, watching drinkers come and go and seeing dusk darken to night.

He must have seen the barman on the phone, must have seen The Ox come in, two guys flanking him. And he must have seen the drinkers leave and the barman lock the door behind them.

Occhi turned to The Ox. "I don't have it."

"Your brother has it."

"No."

"Where is he?"

"May I see Don Strachi?"

"He gives his respects."

✳ ✳ ✳

The cop walking the night post on Third Avenue stayed mostly bored through the quiet hours. Rain had stopped, but his rain gear, the sidewalks and streets still glistened wet.

In a lumberyard littered with timber scraps and shredded billboards, a peacoat draped a barrel that the cop had not seen earlier. He stepped to it, lifted the coat, and staggered back from a face with eyes this way and that, staring out from a muck of sawdust and blood.

The cop called it in; Central called Joe; Joe got out of the sack and to the scene about the same time the sun did. People stood at windows watching cops shuffle barricades, and a detective stoop under his camera's darkening drape.

"Make sure to show the eyes," Joe said.

From under the cloth the photographer said: "You got here fast, Joe."

"And what do you think?"

"Already I got the eyes, got the piece of paper in his mouth. And got a whiff of that guinea red. I mean, you know, wine."

The photographer flicked the cloth off his shoulders and squeezed the shutter bulb. "All done."

Joe called to the uniform guys: "Knocking on doors?"

"Doing it now."

"I need reports right away."

"Okay, Boss."

"Get some of this saw dust."

The photographer collapsed his tripod, lifted it to his shoulder. "This handsome fella's all yours."

Joe lifted a short corner of the paper from Occhi's lips, read its message — *To never again write knife letters* — written clearly on an invoice of Enzo Burgundi's tailor shop.

He ran it to the Squad room, got on the phone.

"Yeah."

"Benny there?"

"No."

"Tell him to call his uncle."

"Wait, here he is."

"Hello."

"What do you know?"

"Last night, nine, ten o'clock," Benny said. "*La Stella di Napuli.*"

"How'd they find him?"

"He found them. Showed up there looking for Strachi."

"Who did it?"

"Who do you think?"

"No, who do you think?"

"Had to be ... you know."

"What is it I know?"

"They kill the tailor. Occhi and the brother get on a lam. Then Occhi ends up in a barrel and word moves around that Strachi's a swell guy for making revenge, and the swell guy gets respect."

"Who's talking to you?"

"The Ox. Who else?"

"He was there?"

"He says no, but he's been off the wine and his tongue is tight."

"The fingers," Joe said.

"What, the fingers?"

"Cut off one hand."

"No shit. Trying to get that painting out of him."

"Did he give it up?" Joe asked.

"Nobody's saying."

"When did you see The Ox?"

"I didn't. He called me before about the olive oil, told me

don't go far. Plates for funny money is the thing. Is what it is, I mean."

"Every day, no matter what, you call me. Every day."

"Okay, but how come you're not asking me where the plates are now, who has them, how they getting here? You know, like you ask about the painting."

"Let me get this straight. You ask questions and I answer, or — ?"

"All right, all right, Joe. But you don't ask me because you already know. Right?"

"Where'd the barrel come from?"

"The ones under the bar came from the candy maker. He keeps barrels in the yard there."

"Get a handful of sawdust from the floor."

"They spit in that shit, Joe."

"Call me when you get it."

"Can't you guys get it?"

"Call me when you get it."

East Thirteenth

———

Photos of Black Handers covered the walls of the Italian Squad room. Their knife letters, shaking down yeggs and boosters, madams and pimps, fattened case folders.

But Joe spent most of his worry on the good guys: men with picks and shovels toted like carbines, leaving their families in the dark of mornings, returning in the dark of evenings. He worried for the grocers, shoemakers, barbers and tailors.

And for Ernesto Giacalone, respected landlord of a dozen neighborhood properties. A good man who spent much of the rent money he took in on battling roaches and rats and tolerating rents late and short. He had well earned the privilege for his wife and daughters to live in comfort on their first floor, two bedroom apartment on 11th Street.

He had shown Joe the letter:

Piece of carrion,
    We beg you warmly. We need $7,000. We know that you can sell your buildings and pay it. If you do not leave it in envelopes near your door tomorrow your entire property will be destroyed and then you have to pay the money anyhow.

The landlord ignored the letter, ignored a second one, and days later his family and his tenants woke to a blast that shook and scattered the stoop and vestibule into a rubble of concrete and twisted iron.

"Understand, Giuseppe," Giacalone had said, his face pale and long, "what else is there to do?"

"You will give them their way?" Joe asked.

"They will leave me in peace."

"Give the devil your finger and he will have your hand."

"I will use the other hand. What else would I do? They have bombed the building of my home. Renters are leaving and no one can blame them. If I refuse what they demand, they will steal the building of the tailor's shop, or someone will be killed."

                 ❊ ❊ ❊

The judge who'd signed most of Joe's search warrants read his latest application to search a Thirteenth Street basement apartment. An anonymous phone call about a bomb factory, according to Joe's fourth paragraph, initiated surveillance that corroborated enough of the phone caller's information to apply for the warrant. The judge put the okay on it.

Before daylight, the Squad toted a battering ram to the apartment door, but the door hung open like a welcome.

They went in. The place smelled like sewer. A bare bulb hung from the ceiling, made glare and shadow on a guy on the floor, face down in a smear of blood as wide as his belly, teeth and brains in the blood. A twelve gauge double barrel lay near him. The sewer was in his pants.

Another bomb maker sat on an empty crate stenciled *EXPLOSIVES,* most of him on a table next to a sheet of paper and a list of tenants of Ernesto Giacalone's 11th Street building. Written across it: *To never again write knife letters.*

Back to the Squad room, Joe pulled the Strachi folder. The ball breakers who'd signed the Valentine card had traced a black hand on the folder, made Joe grin.

He opened the folder on his desk, found three knife letters and set them side by side: the one he'd removed from the black jacket in the tailor shop; the message in Occhi's dead lips; the letter Giacalone found under his door; and now the scribble across the list of Giacalone's tenants.

Joe pieced together a new search application letting each letter of different handwritings show conspiracy. Then he plugged in a pattern that linked the Black Hand to the Camorra, to Cesare Strachi.

Philomena Matruzzo One

When Philomena Matruzzo, the strong, contented woman whom Lucia Burgundi envied and respected, got off the boat in 1903, she had no baby and one husband. A year later she had one baby and no husband.

He'd kissed her goodbye one morning after Christmas to work silver mines in the Arizona Territory. She never heard from him again. Not a cent of what he'd promised to send, no concern for his son and, "if he is dead, may he be with God. If he is not dead, he should bust."

Thanks to the saints, she'd had the job before he left — cleaning Christ the King Church and rectory and preparing meals for its priest, Don Camillo. Her pay from the Irish — that's what she called the bishop of the diocese — came every two weeks, but even adding the generosity of Don Camillo to her pay, she owed the bread store, the fish market, the grocer, butcher, and her landlord. Only their patience kept her and the baby Laurio fed and sheltered.

She asked the saints, Anthony and Rocco the most responsive, for Laurio's health and, not for money, but for work to earn money. "Please, just enough to show that I am not a beggar."

She lit fresh candles before each of them — Anthony on the small table near her bed, and Rocco on the shelf over the kitchen sink—and within that week, as she swept the front steps of the church, her landlord, Ernesto Giacalone, offered that she earn her rent by seeing to the halls and toilets of the building where she lived. "Unless it is too difficult," he said apologetically.

Philomena, with eyes black and sharp in a face soft and earnest, said quickly: "No, no, it is not difficult."

So with the baby Laurio bundled in an apple crate with pictures of Indians and teepees pasted to its sides, she scrubbed the five stories of floors and stairs on hands and knees.

Giacalone saw this and said: "Philomena, the mop, use the mop."

Philomena kept scrubbing. "It is not so good as the brush."

"If you use the mop you will have the time for another building."

Now she stopped and looked up. "For you? For pay?"

"For pay, of course."

❊ ❊ ❊

Philomena paid all she owed, got herself a bankbook, and whenever she walked into the bank with a few coins to deposit, she stepped proudly, smiling for the tellers, who greeted her with nods and said: "Good day, *Signora*."

She bought a small silver medal of San Gennaro, had Don Camillo bless it and, each time she pinned it on something of Laurio's clothing, she admonished the silver saint, the wooden Anthony and the plaster Rocco. "He will be a priest, this baby. You must see to that."

It was not until October, months before the knife letter to Lucia, that Philomena became distracted, first by dreams of Laurio as a young priest wearing a black jacket, and then by seeing a priest she didn't know walk into the tailor shop wearing that jacket.

Later, from her window, she watched him, no longer wearing the jacket, shake hands with the tailor in front of the shop, then walk past the Patarama Stable and out of sight. The next day she saw the jacket — a fine, handsome one, she thought — on the clothes dummy in the tailor's window.

After some days, the jacket still in the window, Philomena asked Lucia about it.

"A fine garment," Lucia said. "Not one that should be forgotten. But the priest has not returned, though he has asked that Enzo rush to repair a tear."

"Don Camillo knows nothing of him," Philomena said. "What do you know?"

"Only that he is Sardinian, and that someone will see his jacket in the window, inquire of it, and will pay us for our trouble."

Not Lucia, and perhaps not the tailor knew as much about the jacket as did Philomena, because in her latest dreams its pockets ballooned like full stomachs and overflowed with gems and gold she'd seen only in magazines and moving picture shows.

The Murder Stable

Arnie The Swede, twenty-three years old, wore the same plaid shirt and brown tie every day. He stood tall and slim, with eyes blue and soft, and never wore a hat to cover his head topped with a scatter of nearly white hair. He had a pretty wife and they lived with their baby boy in the apartment over their *Portraits and Miniatures Studio* on the Bowery.

Before Headquarters had a Photographs and Records Department, *Portraits and Miniatures* contracted for prisoners' mug shots on the way from booking to arraignment. Arnie got to know cops and cop talk. He liked these gritty men, felt comfortable with them and, as a matter of business, so he told his wife, spent an occasional evening with them in gin mills around Headquarters.

That was how he got word of the search warrant and why he left his home at first light, camera and tripod on a shoulder, headed for the Patarama Stable.

The day already hot and damp, he got there in time to watch Joe and the Squad, in old clothes and overalls, get there in a paddy wagon that cops and prisoners called a Black Maria, carrying shotguns and battery lanterns. Three uniform cops from the reserve platoon sat with them. Three other cops and a sergeant rode in a sanitation truck pulled double harness.

They all rolled into the stable gate onto a rutted driveway that elbowed to the rear yard, where sections of roofs, panels, buggies and carriages made pyramids among the rusty remains of a sled on runners and leaf springs. Three or four sheep huddled where oak wheels hung on a plank fence; a keg of horseshoe nails, an anvil, and lengths of chain lay in a crop of poison ivy.

Out of the stable burst a flurry of chickens and Fausto Patarama, a growl in his throat and a pinch bar in his bear-like hands.

A detective leveled a shotgun at Patarama's face. He dropped the bar, but then kicked like a horse, shook off night-sticks and blackjacks, and whined like a cat when they cuffed him to a rabbit hutch.

"Like a dead dog he stinks," one of the cops said.

One of Fausto's sons, small, skinny and slow, brown curls on his head falling over his ears, held a young rabbit in his arms, kindness in one of his eyes, and zeroes in the other. He didn't fight and he didn't stink, just waved to his shackled father as detectives sat him and the rabbit on a milk can.

"What's your name?" Joe asked.

"Apollo."

"You have a last name?"

"Yes."

"What is it?"

"You are Petrosino?"

"Yes."

"I am stupid and I must not talk with you." He curled his lips against his teeth.

"Where are your brothers?" Joe asked.

"I am stupid and I must not talk with Petrosino."

"Who killed Occhi?"

"He is killed?"

"Yes."

"He is stupid, too."

"Why is he stupid?"

"He did not find the painting, but maybe he did."

"You have seen the painting?"

"No."

"Who wants it?"

"Everybody."

"Where did he look for it?"

"The tailor."

"Where is the tailor?"

Gaga looked away, put all of a thumb into his mouth.

"Who has the painting?"

"Nobody," he mumbled, thumb still in his mouth.

"Did Occhi have it?"

Gaga shrugged.

"Does Carlo have it?"

Gaga shrugged.

People climbed from flats onto the zigzag of fire escapes to look down on the stable. A crowd at the top of the driveway thickened when an ambulance and a morgue wagon parked on the street.

The uniform sergeant saw Arnie in the crowd and tapped a cop's shoulder. "On the gate, and don't be letting in no newspaper people. And tell that Swede fella up there we don't need no pictures today and I'll be pleased not to see him again."

The detectives hauled shovels, picks and axes from the sanitation truck into the stable. Beneath skeletons of buggies and coaches, a floor of limestone rectangles squared itself against the earth that extended under to the stone and masonry wall with the door in it.

The dust of stable shit kicked up as the detectives walked to the stalls of horses and a mule, none badly tended. A nervous goat stood with the mule.

The men opened the stalls and the beasts, as if they'd been waiting for the moment, cantered into the yard, broke through the crowd at the gate, and scattered into the street. The mule wandered stupidly, a butcher in a bloody apron eyeing the goat at the mule's haunches.

The first swings of a pick into the ground cut loose a stench. Somebody called the morgue's wagon into the yard and the uniformed guys unloaded bottles of ammonia and chlorine. They poured gallons around the shallow grave, then another grave, and then others, but it did little to weaken the reek that grabbed onto the humidity and leeched to the street.

They dug into three graves, found seven bodies, one of them almost fresh.

Joe called to Gaga: "Come here to see."

Gaga stood, moved the baby rabbit to one hand, covered his nose and mouth with the other, and shuffled to where Joe was pointing.

"He is the tailor," Gaga said.

"From up the stairs?"

"Yes."

"Did he have the painting?"

"I don't know."

"Who are the others?"

Gaga shrugged.

"How did they get here?"

"They died."

"Who brought them?"

"I did not see."

"Did you see Don Strachi?"

"I do not know who that is."

"Or The Ox?"

"No ox."

"Is the painting here?"

"I do not know."

The morgue guys loaded their wagon with crates and sacks of what was left of seven victims.

The digs that had buried the bodies and the new dig sent an inside wall into tilt and ruptured a gas line, but the open doors and gabled windows kept the odorless vapors harmless.

The sun set, dark settled in, and the detectives scrambled into the wagons and trucks, taking with them two stilettos, a .30 caliber rifle, a 12 gauge, double barreled, sawed off shotgun, a box of buckshot, pieces of seven bodies, and no connection to Cesare Strachi.

Joe said to the uniform sergeant: "Tomorrow morning same time. That good?"

"Good by me, Joe."

❊ ❊ ❊

The search would resume in the morning, into closets, cabinets and desks on floors that sagged under paper-packed lockers and chests. There could be something in that mess — a phone number, an address, anything that connected Strachi to the stable. And maybe a painting stashed in a place too dark for Lina to see.

A fresh squad of reserves got to the stable to keep it secure. The stink, new to their noses, twisted their faces.

They'd been told to let no reporters past the stable's gateway.

But Arnie the Swede, who seemed to get there for the first

time that day, was not a reporter. So the cop at the sidewalk gate said *sure Arn*ie, and the cop at the stable doors said the same.

Arnie mounted the camera on the tripod, set the lens, loaded flash powder, and fought gags as he quick-stepped into the stable. Holding his breath, he fixed the tripod's legs, aimed the camera into the dark, opened the shutter and sparked the flash powder.

The blast singed off the fumes of death. The stone wall stood sturdy because the explosion tore at the roof and sent it climbing, tearing, then falling in rubbles of lumber and slate to the stable floor and on the smolder that used to be Arnie the Swede.

※ ※ ※

For years, Joe Petrosino had been going to the restaurant on Spring Street for Vincent Saulino's good food, and for Adelina, Saulino's widowed daughter. But at the end of this long day, with the stink of death lingering in his nose, the aches in his head, and any possible connection to Cesare Strachi burned up or blown through the stable's roof, the attraction was the wine.

At his regular table, Joe sipped from the glass that Adelina had filled before she brought the fish and potatoes. With sleepy eyes Joe followed her move from table to table, wearing the dress he liked. A simple dress, a print with flowers and yellow stems, and a white apron, still new. She'd done some woman magic with her black hair, her lips, her cheeks. Or maybe he had never noticed.

There had been no thunderbolt with Adelina as there had been with Lucia. No dreams and no longings, and though thoughts of her pleased him as much as any woman who had ever caught his eye, thoughts for Lucia still triggered his fantasies.

Adelina filled his glass again, took off the apron, and sat across from him. Looking at his plate, she asked: "You are not so hungry, or you don't like?"

"No, it's good. I'm tired, that's all."

"You work too hard for the police."

"Maybe."

"Never I see you too tired to eat. There are troubles, I think."

"You think so?" He grinned.

"There is danger and it is why you care to not have a wife."

Joe chuckled, kept a smile. "I am too busy for a wife."

"Papa says you soon will retire and rest."

"I cannot allow *malavita* the joy of seeing me retire."

"I too will have joy to worry no longer for you."

Joe leaned forward, a hand on the table. "You worry for me?"

Adelina set both her palms on his hand. "You choose not to see that I do."

"You worry for danger?"

"Yes, and that you are alone."

"I am rarely alone, Adelina." Joe took back his hand and forked a piece of fish from his plate. "My job does not allow loneliness."

"Your job is not a home."

"Only with a wife will I have a home? Is that what you say?"

"It is what I say."

"And a meal like this every night?" Through a smile he filled his mouth with a roasted potato.

"First you don't eat, Giuseppe. Now you eat too fast."

Heat Wave

The gift of Don Cesare's roses without perfume had gone limp, but now a perky and fragrant bouquet, delivered from the florist next door, filled the vase and made Lucia smile as she stepped to the back room with the lunch of peppers and eggs she and Rosina had prepared that morning. She set the lunch in the ice box, opened the rear door, lifted the window over the sink, then switched on the ceiling fan.

With the fan's breeze rustling pages of *Mondo Nuovo* on the small desk, she sat, worn with four months of baby in her belly, and cranky with heat that had arrived these early weeks of summer.

She opened the top of her dress and sponged her neck and shoulders as she read new *Mondo Nuovo* and *Il Progresso* columns of the stable fire, now two weeks old, the identified and unidentified bodies, and the indictment of Fausto Patarama.

News of the heat wave, on the same page of *Il Progresso*, seemed a related story. Ninety degrees and one hundred percent humidity. There had been sunstrokes. Horses collapsed in the streets. Crowds mobbed Coney Island for days, many sleeping on the beach through the night. Items about mattresses and pillows on tenement roofs and fire escapes she didn't read. That was not news.

And she didn't have to read that ice had become scarce. No delivery in two days. Fish rotted, complained the fish man. Butchers tossed decaying meat to roaming dogs before rot got to stink.

She heard the *calabrese* come into the shop and bark about his fruits and vegetables going to waste. She fixed her dress and stepped out to see a sack of peaches on the work table.

"Before these go bad, too," the *calabrese* said, looking from Rosina to Lucia. Even with the heat, he kept a cap on his head, removing it almost rhythmically to dab a limp red handkerchief on his climbing forehead.

"The saints allow us to suffer," he said, his voice angry, a finger pointing to the heavens, "and I forbid my wife the coins to light candles."

"But we thank the saints because they have sent you to help us through the day," Rosina said. "How worse it would be without them."

"Yes, yes," the man said through a sigh. "This heat will end." He wiped his face, bunched the handkerchief into a hip pocket and turned to leave.

"Thank you for the peaches," Rosina said.

Lucia rolled her eyes and yawned through a smile. She and Rosina had been up during recent nights in their airless flat, sponging themselves at the kitchen sink.

"It has never been like this," Lucia said, moving a chair to the pattern table and sitting across from Rosina.

"Perhaps we should stay here tonight," Rosina said. "The fans are a help."

"I have thought the same and thought too to have the coffin here." She gazed through thoughts that hardened her face. "I thought it was over, but he's still a bother. Dead, and still a bother."

"Sister, no more, please. It will be over soon."

"Yes, yes, very well," Lucia said.

Rosina took the peaches to the back, washed and sliced them, and tasted one. Stepping out, she said: "The *calabrese* has made a truly sweet gesture. We must be sure to — "

She was interrupted by Benny Bats. He'd come into the shop with steps as snappy as his words. "Signora, I offer late condolences for your troubles. I did not know your husband well, but I believe he was a fine man."

"My sister is the widow," Rosina said, looking to Lucia.

Benny turned to Lucia as if first seeing her.

"Excuse me, I am confused."

Lucia heard no American accent in his *napulitan'*. "Thank you for your kindness," she said.

"I am Benito Carlucco, associate of Don Cesare Strachi, who wishes to inform you that the sale of this property is complete and he is pleased to be your landlord."

"Yes, Giacalone has told us," Lucia said. "Are we to expect changes?"

"I know only what Don Strachi has already told you, Signora. No need for worry."

"Worry comes easily to my sister and me."

Benny looked again at Rosina, caught her looking at him. He smiled, she smiled, and he said: "But perhaps you will interrupt doubt so that we can see to a suit."

"For you?" Lucia asked.

"For me, yes."

Lucia stepped back and scanned the suit he wore, the shirt, the collar. "Very well," she said to Rosina, "we must fit a suit for Mr. Carlucco."

"So pretty are ladies when they smile," Benny said and both women smiled. "And I see you have received my flowers."

"Yes, thank you, they are beautiful. There was no card, we did not know from who ..."

"I just wanted you to have them."

"We thank you."

"Now for the suit?"

"You wear a fine suit now," Lucia said. "A good material for summer, an elegant cut, clean stitching."

"It is wise to please Don Cesare, who is particular about the appearance of those who work for him."

"Double breasted? Single?"

"One of each?"

"Dark colors? A summer flannel, worsted?"

"Worsted would make a fine figure for business."

He looked to Rosina, Lucia watching her find Benny's gaze.

"Rosina, please show Mr. Carlucco our patterns."

Rosina plopped catalogs on the counter and flipped the pages to sketches of suits. Benny chose one, then another, and agreed with the fabrics and colors the sisters suggested.

Lucia's worth in the business had been her hands, stitching so precise as to appear part of the fabric. Enzo had said that, praising her, but praising himself, because he had taught her. Taught her too, with unusual patience, how to measure each length and width, to always consider the figure of the customer and to insist that he or she wear the work and remain as still as the clothes dummy in the window while she pinned bodices and hems.

He had not allowed his wife to measure a man, but she'd watched and found no trouble imitating him. She could have asked this handsome man to supply her with a suit that fit him well. The suit he wore would have given her all the measurements she needed.

"Remove your jacket, please," she said and glanced at Rosina, her face bright for Mr. Carlucco. Lucia handed the tape measure to her, and stepped back.

Rosina hesitated, but then handled the tape measure more certainly than being new at it, calling out numbers for Lucia to record. Neck size — *his collar fresh, a scar on the side of his face she'd not noticed before* — shoulders and chest, waist and hips — *like an eel, but sturdy*.

"Step on the fitting platform please," Rosina said, then watching in the looking glass, had him turn and turn again. "Do you wear shoes like this always?"

"Yes."

"Stand straight please."

"This is straight as I get," he said with a grin.

"Fine," Rosina said and, with snaps of the tape, measured the arms, shoulders and waist, the legs from waist to cuff, then faltered at the in-seam measurement. But with Lucia watching, challenging, the younger sister set the tape and called out a number.

"It will be a minute to make a price," Lucia said.

"That's all right, whatever it is. You'll be as honest as your husband."

"You have been here?"

"Yes," Benny said. "As I say, I knew him not well, but he corrected the lengths of my sleeves after a tailor on Hanover Square made the suit."

Lucia looked to his jacket draped on a chair. "I do not recall ..."

"Not this suit, another," he said.

"With so many tailors here, why go there?"

"He was a *paesano* of my father's and was kind to me and mama when my Papa died in the snow of '88."

"We have heard of the snow. I am sorry."

"As I am sorry for your loss. They say there was a knife letter, and that their real concern was for a work of art."

"Work of art?"

"Yes, a valuable painting that had been stored here during negotiations of a sale."

"Perhaps that is why the shop was in such upset. But no work of art has ever been in this shop."

"Very well, Signora, but you should know that its return would result in a substantial reward."

"Enzo never spoke of a painting. I hope that it causes no further problems for us."

"That is doubtful. Don Cesare's associates are not threatened by thieves or knife letters."

"We are not associates. We are renters."

"But renters of a Don Cesare property."

Lucia helped Benny with his jacket.

"When may I return?" he asked.

"Tuesday would be good. For a fitting."

"You'll get to it that quickly?"

"My sister and I spend much time in the shop."

"There are so many tailors," Benny said, with a look of concern, "profit must be difficult."

"As long as we have hands, there is profit enough."

"Don Cesare is concerned for your troubles and it would please him to assist you with the expense of the funeral home."

"Thank you, but our neighbors have suggested the shop for its room and cooler air."

Rosina looked away from the lie.

"You have contacted an undertaker?" Benny asked.

"We have yet to hear from the morgue."

"An unpleasant detail."

"Please tell Mr. Strachi that I thank his gesture and will consider his offer of kindness."

Benny dropped bills on the work table and stepped toward the door. "I look forward to seeing you ladies again."

❖ ❖ ❖

Benny walked out of the shop, letting go a hint of a limp that usually softened up women. This time it helped the lie that he knew nothing of what Strachi was up to, why he'd strong armed Giacalone's building, or why he needed to buy the scorched lots of ground where the stable used to stand.

The Ox had called Benny. "He wants us to meet him."

"For what?" Benny asked.

"I don't know."

"Where?"

"I'll come get you."

An hour later the three of them stood in the litter of ashes and charred remnants of the stable. Strachi's shirt was bright in the midday sun, his thumbs tucked behind black suspenders.

"What should we do with this?" he asked, twisting and looking around.

"I don't know," The Ox said. "What?"

Strachi looked to Benny. "You. What do we do with this?"

"I don't know, Don Cesare."

"What else but make another place for the dead?"

"A cemetery?" The Ox asked.

Strachi grunted. "What do you say?" he asked Benny.

"A funeral parlor?"

"Yes." Strachi put an arm around Benny's shoulders. "A business that sells sorrow and privacy that even the ignorant police would not disturb."

"But what do we know of the business?" The Ox asked.

"That it needs an undertaker."

"But that is not all."

"Of course, that is not all. But an undertaker indebted to us. Who will it be, Ox?"

"I don't know."

"You don't know our friend with the shovel and the warrant of arrest?"

"The Digger is a carpenter," The Ox said.

"And what else does he do?"

"Makes coffins?"

"And what else?"

"He steals from the dead."

"So, he's an undertaker," Strachi said with a laugh and a cackle.

Zella, Gaga, and the Digger

The Digger was Marcello Ulino, a loose limbed man with a long face that grinned on its own. Doctors had told him that nerves and muscles, not the devil, made his face happy. A priest agreed and splashed him with holy water.

He'd grown a moustache, let it grow to droop into a frown, but stares of people who did not know him and some who did, like his wife and sons, wouldn't let him forget the look of a feeble mind on his face.

The letter he'd been waiting for found its way to the dusty side of the mountain where his house had stood for centuries of Ulinos. The letter told him that, "the penal order could not be stopped. We are waiting for you." Nothing, he knew, to do with stealing graves, but all to do with the dishonor of a child.

He rolled out of bed in the middle of a night, woke his wife, handed her a fold of lire and kissed her cheek.

"Soon you will come to America," he told her, then lifted an old ammo crate that held his carpentry tools and papers onto his shoulder. He walked hours to the Mediterranean and boarded a fishing boat that took him to a cattle boat noisy with men and boys speaking Portuguese.

Before the boat left the Mediterranean and all around him was black, he stood at the rail and snapped open the lock on the box. From it he took a tintype of himself, his wife and boys, tossed it into the salted wind, blessed himself, and wondered as to his importance to Don Cesare, cousin to both his mother and his father, having directed him to stay with Zella, the old woman.

In the neighborhood before fire escapes, garbage pickup and indoor plumbing, Zella's eyes stayed black and polished as the rosary beads that hung on the wall at the head of her bed. The line under her bony nose was her mouth and it smiled on one side and frowned on the other.

Never without a kerchief to hide patches of scalp under her kinky gray hair, she spent afternoons at her kitchen window on the alley, mending children's clothes that she gave to one society or another.

Before Georgie Nuts made his first drop for Benny, the two of them went to Zella. Benny looked sharp in a derby, fresh collar and cuffs, and a suit by the sisters. Georgie, in his beat up corduroy jacket, looked slow.

Zella raised her window when she saw them. She took off silver rimmed glasses, cleaned them with her apron, and put them back on her face.

"The undertaker, how the hell did he get in here?" she asked Benny.

"The Ox."

"What's his name?"

"Ulino, Marcello."

"The son of a bitch scared the shit out of me this morning," Zella said. "Looks like he's the one that needs a coffin."

"Where is he?"

"In bed." She looked to Georgie. "And this is Giorgio with the nuts?"

"The peanuts," Georgie said, bowing a bit.

"Tonight you start?"

"Yes."

"He knows what to do?" she asked Benny.

"He knows."

"The key, he has it?"

"I got it," Georgie said.

"Come closer, let me see you." She took off her glasses, cleaned them again. "Why I never see you before?"

"I never saw you either." Georgie smiled, and it looked like she smiled back.

"You are chubby. You are married?"

"Yes."

"Kids?"

"Five."

"You talk American?" she asked in English.

"Sure," Georgie said.

"You always wear that jacket?"

"Sometimes."

"You look like a greenhorn. Bring peanuts when you come."

❋ ❋ ❋

The next few mornings Zella found a sack of peanuts on her kitchen table and one morning found a kid sucking his thumb and staring into the window.

"*Guaglion'*, what you do there?"

"Where I live is burned."

"You are a boy of the stable?"

"I am Apollo."

"Someone brought you here?"

"For eat, and for work."

"Who brought you?"

"He gave me nuts and nickels."

"Are those all the clothes you have?"

"Yes."

"No socks?"

"Nobody gave me."

"How many years you have?"

"Fifteen."

"You are small if you are fifteen. You go to school?"

"No school. I am strong."

"You have seen death?"

"Yes."

"Do the dead come to you?"

"No."

"Do you speak American?"

"Yes. Eat now?"

Zella mumbled: "Another one they send me."

"What?"

"You want work?"

"I am strong."

"Come in."

The soles of Gaga's shoes, hinged where stitching had not rotted away, slapped the linoleum on Zella's kitchen floor. If he was strong, he didn't look it. Skin and bones. Maybe stupid and maybe not, something going on behind big black eyes under his head of curls the color of old pennies.

She began filling the counter tub and handed him a bar of brown soap. "Do you know what this is?"

"For wash."

"Do you have bugs?"

He shrugged.

She rummaged his curls. "No bugs. Now wash. When you finish, leave the water. I'll wash those filthy clothes and fix what I can. I don't know how the hell you wear filth like that."

* * *

Zella put a bowl on the table in front of the boy. Hard boiled eggs crumbled over *Polenta*, and a loaf of bread. He ate, watching Zella and The Digger Ulino penciling ads for the newspapers: *Carpentry, Bureaus, Chests, Chairs and Tables ...*

"Enough of that," Zella snapped. "The other thing."

"You think?"

"What do you think you're here for?"

... Coffins of Fine Hardwoods.

"This boy here," she said, "he is not so stupid as he looks. He will work with you. Buy him a coat. And he needs shoes."

"Socks," Gaga said.

"I have socks for him," Zella said.

The Digger looked over the boy. "He will work? He is so small."

"I am fifteen. I am strong." He emptied his bowl, held on to the spoon. "There is more?"

"You had enough," Zella said and took his plate to the sink. She looked to The Digger.

"Underwear too, he needs," Zella said. "He has no family. He will stay with you. Teach him and see that he keeps himself."

The Digger tugged at a corner of his moustache.

"Soon you will see to the arrangements of the tailor," Zella said. "They told you of the tailor?"

"I know, yes," The Digger said.

"Gaga knows too."

"Apollo," Gaga said.

Zella nodded.

"What is the work?" The Digger asked.

"The morgue will carry him to where you will lay him out. That is all you will do."

"And the coffin?"

"It is at the morgue. This they do for us and this you do for Don Strachi."

"When?"

"When you are told. And don't grin when you do it. You look *stunat'*."

Crosses

The day had been hot and cloudy. Rain began as Lucia and Rosina, both in the black taffeta Lucia had admired weeks before, sat in the breeze of one of the shop's ceiling fans, reading the signatures on Mass cards and on store-bought notes of consolation. Lucia stood to return a card to one of the floral arrangements when she saw the morgue wagon jerk to a stop.

Two figures in black — a tall man wearing a suit that fit well and a smile that didn't, and a boy with pants too long — set the coffin on a wheeled carrier and brought it in.

"I am Marcello Ulino," the man said, his voice not as happy as his face. "I am sorry for your loss and circumstances."

He and the boy lifted the casket to the counter in front of the bins, then the man balled a scrap of flannel and handed it to the boy who stood on a chair and stuffed the wad into the bell at the door to mute the merry sound. The boy seemed to stiffen when the man set his hand at the back of his knee.

"If there are chairs we will arrange them," Ulino said.

"Only the few that you see," Rosina said. "The coffin will remain closed?"

"Yes. The flowers, we will arrange."

"Thank you."

Visitors dropped envelopes of money and Mass cards into

a hand basket on a stool near San Gennaro. Women in black dresses and dark scarves huddled around Lucia.

"How beautiful the flowers," one said.

"The kindness of our people," another said, as the boy from the florist shop brought in a cross of red and white roses, a dazzle in sharp contrast to the gray day. It offered no card, but it did let Lucia recognize both the sender and another cross, colorless and shapeless, intended to linger long after the whites and reds had fallen gray.

The shop filled with familiar faces, some in suits and dresses that Enzo and she had tailored. She knew some of the others, one of them the large Armando Peppone, communist organizer, publisher and editor of *Mondo Nuovo*. He wore his suit of white flannel with a black tie on a shirt wrinkled with humidity and perspiration. Peppone occasionally had delivered his newspaper to trigger political arguments with Enzo.

The man's face, usually red and bright, showed sadness to Lucia. She didn't care for him, his presence intrusive, probing. Weeks past he had come into the shop with a box of pastries.

"Signora, I offer condolences and the services I or *Mondo Nuovo* can provide," he'd said with a shallow voice. "I have been missing the talks with your husband. We agreed little in matters of history and politics, but we respected each other."

"He spoke well of you."

"He appreciated music and the master painters, about which I could offer little."

Lucia had heard Enzo and Joe Petrosino discuss the opera and the arias that the peasants of the Mezzogiorno had sung in the fields, the plazas, and in their homes. But she'd never heard Enzo talk of paintings.

Peppone said: "In fact, he claimed to be the caretaker of a particular work."

"Oh, yes?"

"Yes. Has no one inquired of a painting?"

If Peppone had not asked, she would not have remembered that Benny Carlucco had mentioned a painting.

"No one has asked," she said, and lost sight of the fat man as he stepped to the door.

So Many Rescues

———

Lucia was thirteen years old, attracting the smiles and glances of the men and boys who worked the DiStasi farm, one of them a day worker, an Algerian with teeth black and broken, skin the color of smoke, and the pale eyes of a lost spirit.

At the end of a summer day, Lucia set home through a field that kept the caretaker cottage apart from the DiStasi home, and came across the Algerian sitting on the ground, his back against a wheel of the tool wagon. She did not like this man.

He called to her, but she pretended not to hear and kept walking. She felt him come up behind her, then step beside her. He'd been a sailor, he said, and in all of the world had never seen a woman so beautiful.

"I am not yet a woman," she said.

He gripped her face to kiss her, she refused. He insisted and they grappled and he threw her to the ground. She screamed and he put his hand over her mouth and bared her and bit her and tore her and she bled and she heard the cottage door and the voice of Cuccio, then saw the black fire of the dog's eyes as his jaws arrested the attacker.

Other dogs responded, Signore DiStasi in his house robe at a run behind them, his shotgun angled before him. As the rapist begged and yelled pitifully, Signore DiStasi left him to the dogs, carried Lucia to the cottage and Mama, and rushed back out.

The frightened sobs of mother and daughter ended at the sound of the shotgun's blast.

"Finut', figlia mi. Finut'." Finished, my daughter. She let her eyes grow wide. "No one must know."

"Mama, I've done wrong?"

"You did no wrong, daughter. But the tongues of gossip make the innocent suffer," she whispered. "That is why no one must know."

No one knew, but Lucia suffered.

Her wedding night, Enzo examined the sheets to find no blood, no evidence of broken virginity. He paced, arms stiff and hands locked behind him, while she sat at the kitchen table, with sobs that wouldn't let her breathe.

"I've done no wrong, Enzo," she cried.

She should have told him before she even got on the boat, he said, should have given him the respect an honorable man deserves. She watched his reflection in the dark of the window, watched the hands at his back open and close.

He stopped pacing, turned and faced her, and with the lifted eyes of a plaster saint, he blessed himself and uttered the moans of a child banished to the limbo that anguished children of *i putan'* must bear. Then he forced himself into her.

❊ ❊ ❊

At dawn on a Sunday morning, she woke with memory bright and thoughts clear. Don Cesare Strachi had freed her from the debts of the viewing, the mass and the burial. He had freed her too of the burden — the cross — of Enzo. Of this she allowed no doubt.

At the kitchen table, a glass of milk, a pencil and paper, words to Don Cesare Strachi seemed to write themselves. *Your benevolence warms me. You have assisted me during difficult times. I vow gratitude.*

She slipped the note into an envelope and stood at the kitchen window looking to where clouds and tenements shared shades of dawn. As a dapple of blue broke from a corner of sky, a group of young women in summer dresses chatted as they passed beneath the window.

One of their dresses reminded Lucia of a wedding dress — not her dress, because it was white. She had seen it in dreams this past week, a night or two after Don Strachi's visit to the shop and his offer of dinner.

"I must finish the work before this day is over," she had said.

"Tomorrow then."

"But the work leaves me so tired, Don Cesare."

She glanced in the looking glass at herself and the growing child due before Christmas.

"Your sister will tend to the shop."

"My sister does more than she should be asked to do. I must not leave her another burden."

Strachi shifted so that window light reflected softly in Lucia's eyes.

"On Sunday —"

"On Sunday too there is work."

"Soon you will begin a life where work does not matter."

"How can that be? There is no life without work."

"I will arrive on Sunday evening to your home. There is no better time than dinner to discuss arrangements I have made."

Still at the kitchen window, she watched a green Cadillac

stop at the curb and The Ox climb from the driver's seat. Except for its soaring canvas roof, the automobile was open, its leather seats polished and inviting. Don Cesare tossed most of a cigar to the gutter and, as The Ox walked into the building, moved from the passenger seat to the back seat.

Lucia heard The Ox climb the stairs and knock on the door.

She kept it closed. "Yes?"

"Don Cesare is here, Signora."

"But I have not agreed."

"Please, Signora."

She opened the door as far as the chain lock allowed. "Must we do what he asks?"

"Please, Signora."

"I must dress," she said but she was lying. She'd already bathed and dressed earlier.

❋ ❋ ❋

Lucia had rarely been in a restaurant, and never one like *Bertolotti's* on West Third Street, out of the neighborhood. Strachi, his hand at her elbow, enjoyed greetings in English and in *napulitan'*, first by waiters, then by a man in a tux and a white carnation, who led them to a round table set for six.

"Others will be with us?" Lucia asked.

"Just us."

"So big a table?"

"It is my table, always available."

"Where is your friend?"

"He prefers to stand at the bar."

"It is how he guards you?"

"He insists."

Feeling out of place became less to do with the careful

glances of men at the bar than with her widow's dress of what she once had thought an attractive material.

She sat and the Camorrista settled his bulk next to her, their backs to a mahogany wall rich with paintings and sconces of glass tinted rosy with gas flames.

She looked to tables where women, unlike any she knew, but American women of sophistication, sat, some with long gloves and flowing gowns trimmed with fine lace. Lively women, some young, some older, accustomed to themselves and to this restaurant. One woman with a cigarette and painted lips wore a gown that Lucia admired, though a chiffon scarf hid much of it. A woman with rings on both hands wore a cascade of pearls over her shoulders. She was speaking with a woman with pale skin and the trousers and shirt of a man.

Strachi well knew his way around the menu, then set it down as if it were yesterday's newspaper. His fingers were manicured, Lucia saw, and each pinky wore a ring.

"Bring what you will," he told a waiter, "but include the veal."

The waiter left, Don Strachi turned to Lucia. "We are here for business, but more importantly, all is well with the child?"

"Yes."

"If I may ask, you have chosen a midwife or a doctor?"

"I have arranged for both."

"As I would have suggested."

The waiter returned with a bottle of wine and a basket of bread. Another waiter delivered a bowl thick with *minestrone* and another of *pasta e fagiol'*. Then plates of *risotto*, of veal cutlets with mushrooms and peas, a beef *pizzaiol'*, then a salad and, finally, a plate mounded with a *zambaglione* custard littered with figs.

They discussed business. She would look after the needs

of Don Cesare's building and shop — "our building" and "our shop," he'd said. She would collect rents and do little else. She would pay no rent, and no gas, electric or telephone bill.

"We have no telephone," she'd said.

"Soon you will."

Lucia was smiling now, letting Don Cesare play with empty talk. She had barely finished a glass of wine, though the bottle was at its bottom. He smiled and she avoided the space in his teeth.

"Consider what I have chosen for you," he said.

"Chosen for me?"

"A shop."

"I don't understand."

"You soon will."

A blush in his face, Strachi held his glass as if studying the rays of light spearing the red wine.

"In the grapes there is truth," he said, setting his eyes on hers. At first soft, they hardened and sparked. He inched his chair closer, shifted and set his hand on the back of her chair. "But I need no wine to assure you that should you give me the honor, in time, of course, you and your child will have my name."

Lucia surprised herself with a near tear. Taking the handkerchief he offered, she promised to consider the unlikely, though despite his looks and grating self importance, he did not frighten her.

He set down his wine and covered her hand with his. The red stone of a pinky ring flared as she took back her hand.

"I have only begun to wear black." She gave back his handkerchief.

He took it with no damage to his smile. "I ask only the chance that your feelings — "

"Please let this be a meeting of business."

"All right, then. To business."

❊ ❊ ❊

The night had turned chilly. The Ox drove up an avenue flanked by brownstones and apartment houses, crossed streets lined with young elms, and lamps lighted with electricity; a neighborhood wrapped in slumber that Lucia knew existed in this city, but had never seen.

The Ox turned into the 24th Street and stopped at a brownstone set behind saplings, squat bushes and iron pickets. He shut the engine and the quiet deepened.

With the soft tones he'd spoken in the restaurant, Strachi said: "This building I have purchased, Lucia. It will make for a comfortable home. Please look."

They faced the house, Strachi saying: "There is an office of real estate suitable for the shop of a tailor. Or a dress shop, as you likely prefer."

"Don Cesare, I don't understand. There is no need. I have a shop. We have discussed arrangements of rent and responsibility, and there is no purpose in discussing another."

"The shop you now have is for your past. This place is your future. A shop, yes, but with a home to accommodate your sister and your baby." He turned to face her and put a hand on her shoulder. "And more babies perhaps."

❊ ❊ ❊

They climbed the dark stairs to her flat and she put her key in the lock. He pulled her to him, she felt power in his arms. She pushed away and he let her, but he grasped her again, firmly but gently.

He locked her face between his palms and put his lips on hers. She responded with curiosity, found warmth and tenderness, but pulled away, leaving his arms angled as if he still held her face.

He turned to the stairs, turned again, a hand on the bannister. He said nothing, but she felt his anger, and if his hat had not tilted comically, she would have been frightened. He turned again and, as the *zuccon'* dropped into his shoulders, stomped down to the darkness.

Though angered, the man had offered no force, no unkindness at her rejections. She found sympathy in the footsteps of his laughable retreat, and certain gratitude to the gentle gangster who had rescued her from the clutches of a less gentle man. And, finally, she found herself smiling at the flowered cross that had lost its duplicity while in the peace of the streets around Madison Square.

Petrosino Does
the Right Thing

A knock at Benny's door. "Come down."

"Be right there."

From his window, Benny looked out on the November day, dry and cool, dust climbing from a street sweeper's broom into the morning slants of sun. A two-horse truck sat at the curb, cases of olive oil on its open bed, and two guys chuting the cases down the sidewalk door into the cellar.

Down the back stairs, Benny went into the rooms behind the grocery, and in the kitchen found the grocer with the Corsican who was with the oil and the horses, a short man with oily hair and moustache. He gabbed some dog Latin that Benny couldn't understand.

The grocer, also a short man, with a clean shirt and apron, handed Benny a paper bag. "Go with him," he said, and dropped a can opener and counter rag into the bag.

Down to the cellar, the sharp smell of old oil climbed from the hard dirt floor to Benny's nose and kept his breath shallow. A bare bulb swinging in a short arc from the ceiling moved shadows along shelves of cans, jars and boxes, and on cases of olive oil stacked four and five high.

The Corsican took Benny to a box that looked like all the others, set it on the floor and stepped back. Benny cut open the box, pulled out the gallon cans, with pictures on them of farms, flowers and maidens.

"Which one?" he asked.

The Corsican shrugged.

Benny opened three of the four cans before he lifted the homemade plates from the olive oil, wrapped them in the counter rag, and set them in the grocery bag. He climbed two and three steps at a time to the hallway phone near his room. He dialed.

"Yeah."

"Ox?"

"Yeah."

"Okay," Benny said.

"They look good? They all there?"

"They're all here. How good, I don't know."

"Stay there."

"When you coming?"

"Now."

"He's with you?"

"Yeah."

Benny called the Squad. "Petrosino there?"

"No. What you got?"

"Plates for twos, fives and tens. US and Canada. They told me wait, they're coming for them. Where's Joe?"

"Near you."

***

When the soles of Georgie Nuts' shoes grew holes, he used to slip cuts of linoleum into them to keep out the sidewalk. But since hooking up with Benny, he wore new shoes. His wife and his kids wore new shoes too. But he kept on the old greenhorn jacket because Benny figured it smart for him to look like a guy who sells peanuts. "You know, a mush, a guy nobody sees."

So Georgie Nuts was in. He kept from getting cocky and stayed calm and sharp when the Black Maria backed into Orchard Street, and Petrosino and his detectives stood in doorways up and down the street. He figured he was getting pinched, tossed betting slips onto the hot coals of the roaster, and turned away players with coins in their fingers, handing them bags of peanuts, saying *not now*.

Across the street the green Cadillac with The Ox at the wheel pulled to the curb, the grocery's sidewalk door still angled open. Strachi, on the passenger side, lit a stogie. The Ox got out, walked to where a harness maker's sign pointed into an alley, and stood there. When Benny came up from the cellar with the shopping bag, The Ox grabbed it.

Petrosino gave the nod, the Maria rolled out of Orchard Street, detectives cuffed The Ox, cuffed Benny, and threw them in the wagon. Joe, Corrao and the counterfeit plates went for Strachi.

Joe said: "Here, don't lose this," and set the shopping bag on the floor at Strachi's feet.

Strachi's face went white, then pink. His jaws tightened. A hollow growl came from his chest. "Turn to blood, Petrosino."

"You know me, *strunz*?"

"Better than you like."

Joe opened the Cadillac's door, grabbed Strachi by the lapels, yanked him out. First the frisk, then jabs and hooks, fists in a blur, arms like pistons. Strachi took it, but buckled.

"Now you know me better, street shit." Joe picked him up, threw him a few more raps, cuffed him. "Anything else you need to say?"

Joe shoved him into the wagon.

Holding open the wagon's door, Joe said: "This automobile, who drives it?" He looked to Benny. "You, what's your name?"

"Benny Carlucco."

"You drive this?"

"Yeah."

"Come on, then."

Benny climbed down, the wagon took off.

"You clobbered the shit out of that fucking scrub, Joe," he said. "What a beating the son of a bitch caught. Like a machine, you did. I heard, but I never believed."

"You could drive this, or what?"

"And no blood. How the fuck ..."

"You could drive this, or no?"

"Yeah."

"Let's go."

"I'm handcuffed, Joe."

They got in the Cadillac, Joe took the cuffs off Benny.

"Where now?" Benny asked. "We wait for night court, right?"

"Court tomorrow morning. The judge is good for us."

"We stay in those fucking Tombs tonight?"

"Where you wanna stay, the Monterey?"

"What I do for you, Joe."

"You do for you, Benny."

"How long we gotta stay in?"

"You and The Ox walk in the morning."

"The Ox walks too?"

"He walks and they think maybe he did the set up."

"And me?"

"They worry about you too. You knew that."

"And Strachi?"

"There's a warrant on the other side for him."

"How the hell did that happen?"

"An election coming up, the Camorra wants their people back in. The paperwork that got buried on the kidnaping that he got sprung for, popped up and they need him back for show."

"Why the hell didn't you just put him on the boat, Joe? *Che cazz'*? Now I gotta worry he's gonna see my two faces."

"Do I tell you don't worry?"

"You do what I do, see if you don't worry. Why the hell did he even show here?"

"You know why. He trusts nobody. That's why he lets nobody know everything. The plates were here for a buyer; he needed to talk about more plates and more money."

"And the buyer was a cop, and that's why you were here before I even called."

"Not a cop. The Secret Service. Their case, we only helped. Unless you testify, they couldn't charge him. I told them you will not testify, so their undercover talked about buying more plates and paper, and that's why the greedy bastard showed."

"You really look out for me, huh?"

"Like you don't know."

"I know Joe, I know. That greaseball Corsican getting locked up?"

"The Secret Service is holding off. And that's good for you. Strachi will think he was the set up. Or the grocer, or the wife. By the time he talks to his lawyer his head will spin so much his mug shot will be a blur."

"And your mug gets in the paper again, yeah?"

"Not your business."

"I got something, but maybe it ain't my business."

"Say what you want."

"Look in Strachi's pockets, maybe there's a picture of you from the newspaper. He keeps it because he's gonna kill you.

Not have somebody else do it. Himself, he says. Okay? I should stay quiet?"

"How long you know this?"

"Yesterday. Got it from The Ox."

"I know it longer than you."

The New Boss

No one made book on who the acting boss would be. All knew that Strachi, cruel and reckless, and Happy Carmine Tonno, cruel and slippery, had grown up on the side of a mountain claimed by generations of Camorra clans that sold muscle, broken knees and murder, and staked the heads of enemies along any piece of road that crossed another.

With a mushroom nose, Carmine Tonno looked like a Sicilian, talked like one when he had to, but his blue eyes from conquering ancestry said other things.

The man's head stayed square no matter what hat sat on it, and usually he wore none. Thick, wavy hair, white since early on. A short stogie in his mouth all the time had tinted his teeth the color of cork. With four or more of his teeth gold, and a few more gone, he rarely smiled, but when he did, the gold glittered like treasure, and made for him the Happy moniker.

The little talk that made it out of his mouth was smart because he was smart — and wise to have a Sicilian wife who had given him four plump daughters and two sons. The younger son was Carmine, Jr., called Mootzi by his sisters when they weren't calling him *piscazot'* — pees his pants — since he'd been in the crib. His brother, Dominic, was another story. From ten years old he held the same blue gaze in his eyes as did his father.

The neighborhood had been home for Carmine since before Strachi got sent there. He never beefed about it, felt that Strachi's operations should have been his, but doing the right thing for the Naples men of respect had paid off for Strachi, so smart soldier Carmine did the right thing too, and stayed patient.

Strachi had made few moves without Happy Carmine's counsel. With the latest bogus money thing, Carmine had warned him. "It feels wrong. Send somebody else, or forget it."

"He's a spender, this guy. He wants to do more things."

"He can't talk to nobody but you? This Benny Bats that you brag about. What about him?"

"All the time you say keep secrets, I don't want nobody knowing too much."

＊ ＊ ＊

That talk with Carmine had been nagging at Strachi since Petrosino kicked him around the street and slammed him in the Tombs. In a damp cell, no blanket, no sunlight, he needed a bath and a shave and his face drooped like a tired sack.

Lying on the iron shelf that was his bed, watching a roach stroll the ceiling, he heard Carmine's *napulitan'* before he saw him. "They're sending you back."

Strachi bounced to his feet, and Carmine almost smiled.

"You saw the lawyer?" Strachi asked.

Carmine nodded.

Strachi sensed a look behind Carmine's face, a look of satisfaction for ignoring his counsel, a look of spite with ideas of making a run at boss.

Strachi gripped the bars of the cell.

"The widow," he said, his voice soft, "she's in the house?"

"Her and the sister, yeah."

"I wrote letters, but nothing came back. She asks for me?"

"She asks if you will return. Asks Benny."

"What do our friends say to that?"

"They are unhappy with your judgment."

"They fault me for being arrested."

"Yes."

"They getting me out?"

"They are not moved to hurry."

"What I do, I do right away. Now I wait. Till when?"

"First the election."

"And if we lose?"

"We do not lose."

Vito Red

The Italian Navy delivered Don Strachi to the Island of San Stefano, a pile of lava just big enough to fit the rock walls of its ancient prison. But lawyers and court tricks got him placed across half of a mile of the Tyrrhenian Sea, to Ventotene, the small, pastel-colored island filled with the scents of caper and rosemary shrubs, where daughters and wives of Roman emperors had been exiled for political misbehavior, to villas of comfort and mystery.

Not too different for the Camorrista. In a terraced room that was never locked, he looked to the sea, saw sunrises and sunsets. He slept between clean sheets, and freely visited the island's homes for a drink or a meal. Or he strolled to the pier, to the boats and ferries and, on a windy morning watched the mail boat deliver Vittorio San Martino.

Strachi watched him walk up the hill. Tall as a jockey, the face of a turtle, eyes bulbous behind glasses too wide for his face. When in his twenties, Vito had organized farm workers in strikes that hurt the owners of estates in *napuli* and *calabria*. On a chase through woods, a half dozen hounds brought him down.

He evaded the horsemen who followed, and caught a merciful but memorable beating before they turned him over to the red-headed strike breaker, Cesare Strachi.

Not much older than Vito, Strachi had laughed at the young-faced communist, pinching his cheek or tugging his hair and saying: "Still you pee your pants, Bolshevik," and delivered him, muddy and bloody, to the *padron'* who had pay-rolled the capture.

Jailed in a shack guarded by dogs, Vito waited for more beatings, or to be killed, but the wife of the *padron'* had him fed, scrubbed, and sent back to Strachi, a rescue that turned him easy on the aristocracy he'd tried to sack. He invented Strachi into a dime novel swashbuckler and won his hero's trust by giving up other organizers and breaking their strikes.

Strachi embraced him. "You are here quickly."

"It is a privilege." Vito had a small voice. "You look well, Don Cesare."

"As well as one can hope."

Speaking softly, they strolled the narrow streets.

"I have been eager to come," Vito said.

"And eager for New York?"

"For unions, I am told."

"Our friends in New York will explain the unions. It will be good for Carmine to see you."

"You will be in New York?"

"In a time."

"And the painting?"

"The Sardinian has become a mystery."

"Do the police ask of the painting?"

"It is as if there is no painting."

"I may go to Peppone?"

"You believe he will tell you more than he has told us?"

"May I try?"

"Measure what you say. The fat man has two faces."

Madison Square

Madison Square. Polish and prestige. The street cleaners and the mailmen looked like class. Cops too. The Broadway Squad, tall guys with helmets, leather gear and brass as polished as their manners, walked ladies and kids across the traffic-clogged avenues from Madison Avenue to Broadway.

Gentlemen with a tilt to their hats carried walking sticks that made them swagger. They smoked half-dollar cigars and kept daughters, wives and mistresses in the latest wasp-waisted dresses that hung exact inches above the swept sidewalks they strolled in search of furniture, art, fashion and gossip.

They gathered in tea rooms fitted with parlor chairs and potted plants, discussing the extravaganzas of Madison Square Garden and the new Hippodrome; the vocal pleasures of Lillian Russell and Marie Dressler; the accomplishments and failures of those not present; and the rumor that soon a new dress shop would open.

"Italians, I'm told."

"Here? Really?"

"Yes."

"Where?"

"In the Twenty-fourth Street."

"Oh, the last of the new houses. The one with the real estate office."

"Yes, and so nicely decorated."

"Those wonderful furnishings go with the house?"

"Yes, they do."

On 24th, just in from Madison, the house began a shoulder-to-shoulder row of brownstones with varnished doors and curtained windows that looked out on front yards with saplings and bushes squared off by swirled iron pickets.

The row broke at Fifth Avenue and mixed with the architectures of old hotels, mansions and townhouses dressed with class and influence.

It was from this avenue that Lucia and Rosina had stepped like greenhorns behind baby Enzo's carriage.

"These homes have clean faces," Rosina said with a laugh and a surge of poetry. "It seems they smile."

"But will they smile for us?" Lucia asked.

"We will cause them to smile."

Their home had a face too, clean and welcoming. Lucia handed Enzo to Rosina and led the way through a vestibule to the front parlor, the dining room and rear parlor, and the kitchen that had been moved from the cellar to make a place for the real estate office that would now be their dress shop.

Oak stairs and bannisters connected the three floors of the house, each group of steps and landings lighted by sconces of pewter and glass.

They climbed to the second floor and four large rooms, empty but for library shelves and the smells of lumber and shellac. Up to the third floor and a bedroom tucked into each of its corners, they chose two rooms next to each other that faced the street.

Enzo would spend nights cribbed in the hall between

their open doors. They looked at the boy now as if for the first time.

"He will grow to be a gentleman in a home such as this," Rosina said, hope and promise in her eyes.

"He is a man, he will get what he wants."

"Not all men get what they want," Rosina said.

"I suppose we will see."

Lucia fluffed the baby's curls with her fingers. "Petrosino says the curls are yours and people will say you are the mother."

"And more scandal." Rosina laughed, covering her mouth with her fingers.

"Sister, a diaper please," Lucia said. "I put six in your bedroom, you will have to wash others."

Philomena Matruzzo Two

Even after the Italian Squad found the tailor's body in a stable grave, and the murderous Camorrista Strachi forced Giacalone to sell the building of Philomena's flat and the tailor shop, Philomena's dreams continued as did her concern for Lucia Burgundi.

"I will miss our visits and walking by and seeing you at work," she had said, holding Laurio.

Lucia took the smiling baby to her arms and kissed his cheek. "The new shop is not far."

"It is not in the neighborhood, it is far," Philomena said. "And Gennaro? Will he move with you?"

"Gennaro was here before the shop and so he will stay."

"And that black jacket, so fine?"

"If someone with interest in it arrives, see that they get it."

"It will stay in the window then?"

"No, you take it. We will take the dummy. If someone inquires of the jacket, you will hear. See to the exchange of money and take for yourself what they give."

Philomena took the jacket from the clothes dummy and left with Laurio and the jacket in her arms. Into her building, she rushed up the four flights to her kitchen. Breathing heavily from the climb, she sat Laurio in his high chair at the table, and searched the jacket's pockets to find not one gem of her dreams. "Nothing," she said to Laurio, then sighed and shrugged and shook off disappointment, telling herself that perhaps the jacket is simply the promise that Laurio will be a priest.

She looked to Rocco on the shelf above the sink and said: "All right, then, that's good. But you understand, I will not yet thank you and the others."

The Mezzogiorno
Social Club

An evening of wine, music and card games ended with philosophy from a Sicilian stranger with a four-string guitar tuned like a banjo.

"What to name the club?" he asked no one, but strummed chords while studying the two dozen or so faces around him. Then, as if with enlightenment, announced that the club be named to reflect the people of the neighborhood, the faces, the sweat, and the love and spirit of Sicily, Napoli and Calabria — the *Mezzogiorno*.

No one agreed, and no one disagreed and, within the week, white and gold stenciling on what used to be the tailor's show window spelled *Mezzogiorno Social Club*.

From behind the letters, San Gennaro still watched the street. Behind the loyal saint, a room, about thirty feet square, had been fitted with a dozen chairs from a dozen kitchens, and three or four tables of different sizes and shapes.

Every pay day, Vito Red sat at one of those tables, taking union dues from men spent by the week's labor, and handed them their pay envelopes. "You want to keep working," he said again and again, "you like a job, then do the right thing."

And doing the right thing, plumbers and carpenters on their own time put in a new kitchen, nobody asking where the stove came from, or the sink and the icebox. Electricians, wood lathers, plasterers and painters did the right thing too, sometimes working through nights and weekends because they believed Vito Red would do the right thing too.

Masons poured a skin of sandy concrete over the cellar's dirt floor, walled in a corner with cement block, and called the small room an office. In the office they set a safe in concrete, hung a padlocked steel door, and stored cash, loan-shark books and gambling slips. Happy Carmine kept eyes on those steady rackets, and kept bigger eyes on Benny Bats and Georgie Nuts, the guys already running the books and figuring the odds.

Benny got in solid with Carmine, but not with Vito Red. He told Georgie that, when he shook hands with Vito, he let go as if the guy's fingers were snakes. Happy Carmine must have known the snakes from way back, and it looked like they didn't bother him.

Strachi had pulled in Vito for his know on unions, shakedowns, strikes and strike busting, and Carmine followed up with The Ox and a squad of muscle and prostitutes planted on the picket lines around the Triangle Shirtwaist Factory.

The whores intimidated wide-eyed young seamstresses and button-holers, mostly Jews and Italians, just off the boat. The whores told the girls: *A buck and a half a week ain't so bad. We ain't union either, you know. Go back to work, honey, before you end up with us.*

The muscle toted bats, jostled the men strikers, and ended the walkout without cracking a head or busting a knee.

The only guy to take punishment was one of the Triangle partners, a weasel who stood a head taller than Vito. Vito slapped him around till the guy planked up the jack for the service and the first month's protection from further strikes and building inspectors.

That was how Vito earned his bones.

In a suit manufactured by the ladies up on Madison Square, this sudden man of respect pranced to the front office of *Mondo Nuovo.* Its floor of oak, well swept, but stained with the black ink of newsprint, snaked a path around a printing press and stacks of shallow alphabet cases, to a desk crowded with books and periodicals, a typewriter, a phone, a pastry box, and the pear shape of Armando Peppone seated in a worn, upholstered parlor chair.

"Peppone," Vito said. "I am Vittorio San Martino."

"Ah, so we meet." Peppone grunted as he struggled out of the chair at the desk, buttoning his suit's white jacket. "When have you arrived?"

"Only weeks."

They shook hands.

"We have met before," Peppone suggested, studying Vito's face. "A rally perhaps? In Rome perhaps?"

It had been Milan, years ago, before Vito hooked up with Strachi, but Vito stayed mute on it. "Possible," he said. "There were so many of us."

"There *are* so many, my friend. It is not over."

"I suppose not," said Vito, turning briefly, scanning a shelf of books and authors that had once meant something to him.

"I expected you sooner," Peppone said. "Coffee, a pastry?"

Peppone's *napulitan'* tongue fell easy on Vito's ears.

"Nothing, thank you."

"So, you please your associates." Peppone smiled, as if approving the strong arming of one his party's unions. "And your interest in the party?"

Vito Red dropped his face into a frown and shook his head. "There is no longer interest."

"So this visit has little to do with politics or unions?"

"You separate the two?" Vito asked, an edge to his voice like the start of an argument. "But no matter, we will discuss personal profit."

"And profit of your associates?"

"If need be."

"Please sit," Peppone said, motioning to a chair next to the desk.

Vito sat.

"We have lost the Sardinian," Peppone said. "I suppose you have heard."

Vito stayed quiet, then said: "Describe this mysterious Sardinian."

"I saw him but once. Here. Not a tall man, about fifty years, stout, walked as if with pain."

"That is my memory of him," Vito said. "And the package?"

"He showed the painting, but would not leave it with me as arranged. He claimed to have a buyer and that our cause would benefit greatly. You knew him?"

"We met before he traveled for the painting."

"A time ago," Peppone said.

"A year."

"You know that he traveled as a priest?"

"Yes. Do the police have interest in him or the painting?"

"Police have not come to me if they do." Peppone opened the box of pastries. "You know of the bodies uncovered in the stable."

"Yes."

"One of them the tailor, who some suggest had possession of the painting," Peppone said, looking quickly away.

"Yes."

"Still, his murder was the result of a Black Hand kidnaping. His shop was searched thoroughly at the time the knife letter was left. If anything was found, no one knows. Unless Don Strachi ..."

"So clearly you speak," Vito Red said, an eyebrow cocked.

Peppone stammered, then recovered. "I have not been advised against speaking with you, by your friends or by my friends."

"I'm told to be cautious of you," Vito said.

"Not to my surprise. But while I am curious as to the fate of the painting, the party views its worth, as I do, but with less interest, now that our unions have otherwise become more secure with success and profit."

"Be that as it may," Vito said with a quick laugh.

"You find that difficult to believe."

Vito shrugged. "No matter. But if one were to look for the painting, where would he begin?"

"The stable fire allows no reasonable speculation."

"It is gone to ashes?"

"If the stablemen had it, yes, and you must know of their fate," Peppone said.

"I know nothing. What do you know?"

Peppone looked into the bakery box. "They seem to be making their pastries smaller and smaller."

"Peppone, where would one look for the painting?" The edge in Vito's voice came and went.

Peppone answered quickly: "The tailor's widow."

"Surely you have spoken with her."

"She claims she knows nothing of it, but what can we expect?"

"Tell me of this lawyer you praise in your newspaper."

"LaGuardia, Fiorello. He assures us he knows nothing of the painting."

"What is his interest with the party?"

"He is sympathetic to the workers, though rejects the label of communist. At times he works for us without fees."

"A dreamer," Vito said.

"A clever politician."

"What is the worth of the painting?"

"Its disappearance has brought the estimate to thousands of international dollars," Peppone said. "But as I say, given the stable blaze — a blunder by the police by all accounts — estimates are meaningless."

"Why do you imply that Don Strachi had interest?"

Peppone nodded and smiled, then put his hand on the telephone. "From this ugly invention come gossips of jealousies and envies. From where the voices come I rarely have need to know."

Vito stood.

Peppone stood. "We will talk again. For matters of personal profit, we agree?"

"Yes, of course."

"The communications of this newspaper are at your service, should you seek a means to negotiate a private transaction."

"You speak as if I have the painting," Vito said.

"I speak with the hope that you — that we will have it. Perhaps news in *Mondo Nuovo* about missing works of art would incite some useful results."

Philomena Matruzzo Three

Since the steam shovels cleaned up what was left of the Patarama Stable, *Mondo Nuovo* had been reporting progress of the funeral parlor construction, giving praise to the unions, never mentioning the unions that had been strong-armed from Peppone's comrades.

Peppone wrote the place into a palace, printed a photo of the handsome two-story brick and stucco building, and described the "experienced and compassionate Marcello Ulino" as a licensed and caring funeral director.

The eight parlors, all on the first floor, fitted with chairs and couches on carpets of floral design, encouraged sorrow. In the room labeled *Holy Family Chapel*, a trio of stained glass windows, half a dozen mahogany pews, and statues of Jesus, Mary and Joseph, facilitated the Tuesday night exchange of envelopes, or settle-ups.

Top floor living quarters for The Digger and Gaga looked down at the alley that connected all the rear yards in the block. Front offices looked over the din of trolleys, trucks and wagons, their roars and rumbles muted to the parlors.

The storage room, still with only a small stock of coffins, sat in the basement. Next to it, the preparation room had been installed with lead pipe plumbing, marble counters and sinks, electric refrigerators, and walls of white tile.

The city directory listed the place as the *Ulino Funeral Home.* But to some, despite *Ulino Funeral Home* printed in white on the black awning that extended from the front door to the street, it remained the *Patarama Stable,* and it took little time before it became known as the *Patarama Funeral Home.*

❀ ❀ ❀

Philomena Matruzzo ignored *Mondo Nuovo*'s columns about the funeral parlor, but did read a story about art stolen from museums and studios of Europe, and about recovered art, like Leonardo's *Mona Lisa.* Missing for five years from the *Louvre* in Paris, it showed up in the hands of a man with no demand for a ransom, but with a Christian duty to return the masterpiece.

She found the man interesting. Not a rich man, she conjured, but a man of study and honor. Tall with clear eyes and, wearing the black jacket of her dreams, he looked something like Laurio would likely look when once a priest.

She finished scissoring the article when a knock brought her to the door and a kid with a message to see a man of the club. Philomena had known some of the men, their good-mornings and good-evenings, and she best knew the charming Benny Carlucco. But it was the peculiar Vito Red, with those eyes of a merry-go-round horse, who greeted her and sat with her at a table.

His tone was pleasant, saying that the work she does in the building and in the church may be too much already. "But you live here and perhaps you will allow some hours in the week to clean this club."

She became excited that the saints still thought well of her. "I am busy it is true, but it is difficult to turn work away, and I will begin when you like. Thank you."

Though *malavita*, Vito and the others treated her respectfully and generously, and three days every week she opened
the club, Laurio with her, seated at a table with his breakfast
of milk and honeyed polenta and staring at the broken sounds
of the wireless.

No matter the weather, she turned on the ceiling fans
that mixed the stink of stale cigarettes and stogies with whatever fresh air the front and back doors let in. So easy, those
first hours of each day, horseshoes and steel wheels yet to
begin hammering the street.

She set up coffee, gulped half a cup, then got to sweeping
and mopping and keeping sharp for a coin left on the tables
that the last night's card players may have kindly forgotten.

On Sundays she opened the club, but only to start the
sauce. By the time she and Laurio were at Mass, Philomena
pictured the pot simmering and men visiting with boxes of
pastries, or bottles and jars of wine, then sitting and speaking
in whispers with Happy Carmine Tonno.

Sometimes there had been talk that perhaps she should
not have heard. Of that she remained uninterested, but of things
not mentioned she stayed curious and alert. Like the black
jacket.

The one called The Ox, or Benny Carlucco, or Vito Red, but
usually Vito, keyed her into the cellar office, cool and damp
with its walls of sweating concrete, to clean and to get her pay
from the safe next to the desk.

Philomena never considered herself a lovely woman. No
color in her wide face, she wore no skirts fashioned to decor-
ate the shapely heft of her torso — *Laurio was a big boy don't
forget,* she often explained to a looking glass.

Yet, on a bright day, high sun glaring off the concrete of
the back alley, she followed Vito into the cellar, musty after

days of rain that had ended that morning. Stepping on the floor crowded with tubs, barrels and bottles of the wine makers, she felt Vito touching her. Not with his hands, but with the horse eyes that usually avoided her.

"You work hard, Signora. Perhaps a companion would care to visit with you for a dress one would not wear to clean for others."

"And who would do that?"

"My generosity is not unknown."

"And then what?"

"That is for us to see." Vito grinned now.

"Please, my pay."

"Yes," Vito said, then sat behind the desk. "But please, Signora," he said, spinning the safe's dial. "Say nothing, but I have been contacted by representatives of the Vatican to locate a certain work of art brought here by one of their priests for the benefit of so many poor people, who, like you, show dedication to the Church and Our Lord."

Looking into Philomena's face, he took the envelope with her pay and held it in his hand.

"Saint Anthony will help you find it," she said.

"Signora, you knew the tailor, who had knowledge of the art, and perhaps you have gained some knowledge of it too."

"I have not."

"A handsome reward is likely for the good person who helps return it to its true owners."

"It is sad that I know nothing," she said, but felt a sense that soon she would. "My pay please."

In Case the Zuccon' Gets Back

—

When Lucia left the neighborhood for Madison Square, jealousy, envy and tongues of gossip that reached Joe Petrosino's ears, turned the thunder in his chest to acid.

Still, wearing a new bow tie, new collar and bowler, and carrying a box of chocolates under his arm, he walked into the dress shop. He looked quickly to Enzo asleep, his head of curls like those of his aunt Rosina, so black against the scrubbed sheets he slept in.

"A beautiful child," he said, staring at the baby till Lucia stood from the work table to take the candy box from Joe's hand.

"The chocolates I love, Giuseppe."

"Yes, I know," he said, his smile shy.

"You are so good," she said, smiling warmly, and kissing his cheek. "I have veal and peppers warming in the back. I'll fix you some."

"No, no thank you. I came only to visit quickly."

"It is good that you visit. We have seen too little of you."

Joe felt tiny, stinging beads of sweat at the back of his neck. He took a handkerchief from his pocket. "I have hesitated to consider that you would accompany me to a dinner and to the opera, but now I have decided to ask you." He felt his face wearing the smile of a child and he got rid of it with the help of the handkerchief.

Lucia had been keeping her own warm smile, but now her face saddened, and her eyes went soft. She set the box of chocolates on the table. "You are kind, Giuseppe, but if I were to accompany you, I would allow you to think that my affection for you is as yours seems for me. I can have no interest in any man, not even one as fine as you."

"Is that not difficult to say?" If Joe had allowed a second, he would not have spoken. But disappointment and embarrassment triggered his tongue.

"What do you mean?" Lucia asked, not with a challenge.

"I am sorry. I had no intention ..."

"I have done nothing scandalous."

Joe believed her. His gaze froze on her gaze, both of them confused, it seemed, needing something to understand. Perhaps she hadn't read his intentions. He gathered words to complete his offer, explain the honor, but honor became muddled, words stumbled and fell.

The phone rang, Lucia ignored it to speak words of well wishes that Joe wouldn't remember, his concentration scattered by the ringing telephone and the kiss on his cheek turning cool so quickly.

✤ ✤ ✤

Looking back on that day, Joe realized that he and Strachi had been wooing the same woman and, from thousands of miles away, the Camorrista, his power, money, and the house in Madison Square, had overcome the good senses of the good woman.

Benny Bats had told Joe of no strong arm, no threats, nothing but intentions as good as Strachi could provide.

"He says he wants to keep her comfortable, safe, and away from the candy store romeos."

"He told this to you? Or The Ox told you?"

"He did. Strachi."

So that was that. Lucia belonged to Strachi, and Joe could not let himself long for her, visit with her, or interview her without one of his men to lean on.

* * *

Walking down from the squad room with Charlie Corrao, Joe said: "I remind you that Strachi still manages control."

"Of his money interests."

"His interest in the widow."

"And she?"

"Our friend Benny says she is happy in the house, and will stay happy until he gets back."

"And then?"

"Who can say?"

Crossing Mulberry Street, Corrao asked: "He's getting back for sure?"

"We will see," Joe said, shrugging, staring at something far away.

"And Benny stays reliable?"

"Until it suits him not to be. He has become successful. Money, cars, women."

"The widow is one of the women?"

"Benny's eye is for the sister, Rosina. A good woman, loyal to the widow and the baby boy. She worries that the widow cannot manage the baby and worries that she cannot manage the widow."

The men climbed into a beat-up department car, Corrao in the driver's seat.

"Will she resist what we ask?" Corrao asked.

"I don't know, and I don't know how much one influences the other. But Rosina has been cooperative with me."

Corrao drove through darkening streets. Little Italy into Chinatown, into the French Quarter, then past Jews with beards, black hats and coats. North through Little Germany to Park Avenue streets orderly and quiet.

Nearly dark, they parked on Madison Avenue behind a line of hansoms, then walked into Twenty-fourth, Joe under his latest deep derby, and the tall Corrao carrying his hat as if to show off a fresh haircut.

They entered the gate to the brownstone's front yard, Rosina in the window, Lucia at the open door.

"Giuseppe, it is good to see you," she called, smiling.

"Good evening, it is good to see you."

"And this is Detective Corrao, who spoke with us on the telephone?"

"Yes, I am Corrao and I again apologize to disturb your evening."

"Come, we have coffee, and we enjoy visitors," Lucia said, holding the door. "I will take your hat, Detective Corrao. I know Joe likes to keep his, even in the presence of ladies."

"It is something that police seem to do," Corrao said.

"Police with baldness, or all of you?"

Joe had never before heard Lucia wag a darted tongue. Joe looked away from her, let go the hurt, took off his hat.

"A fine home," Corrao said, stepping into the front parlor. "So nice, everything."

"Yes, thank you," Lucia said.

Rosina sat the men at a small table near the window, a pot of coffee, a bottle of anisette, and an electric lamp with soft light.

"The boy is asleep?" Joe asked.

"Yes," Rosina said, smiling. "He fell asleep on my shoulder and I took him to his room. He has his own room now. You must visit when he is awake and see how he is grown."

"You will hear if he cries?" Joe asked.

"We hear," Lucia said. "His cries are for my breast, though I believe he would prefer his aunt's." Lucia stood and stepped to the stairs, climbed the first three or four and stayed there, her head cocked to better listen.

"You must excuse what she says at times," Rosina said softly. "Her thoughts are often not clear."

"She is not improved since the last time you and I spoke?"

"Some days it seems so, but I worry. She says little about it, but she is bitter to suspect she suffers as our mother suffered. And puzzled that your visits have stopped."

"It is difficult to visit," Joe said.

"As I have told her."

"You remain loyal."

"She is my sister."

"The business is good?"

"The customers are pleasant and treat us respectfully. But if the business were more successful, it would perhaps bring peace to her mind. She allows it now to fill with the fear of being tossed to the street."

"And this keeps her in need of Strachi."

"In need to hide her true feelings from him. She fears his return."

"It is why we are here."

"He is to return?"

"It is not unlikely, and we must be prepared. She has heard from him?"

"He sends letters which she does not read."

"There are addresses?"

"The envelopes are blank. Benito Carlucco brings them."

Lucia headed back to her chair, stepping quickly. "We hear if he cries, still we listen carefully," she said, smiling through a long sigh.

"I am afraid we have little time to enjoy this visit," Joe said, "and we must discuss a matter of official importance."

Corrao took an envelope from an inside pocket, set it on the table and flattened a palm on it. "We have photography of an item of business at your old shop."

He opened the envelope and slid the photo into the lamplight. "Please look at it." It was a work order of the old tailor shop, blank, but written across it: *To never again write knife letters*.

"I don't know what this means," Lucia said, looking to Rosina, then to the men.

"I am sorry to say that we obtained this from a murdered man," Joe said, "and it is important to learn all we can of it. The man was Occhi."

"Of the stable?" Lucia asked.

"We think he was responsible for the death of your husband."

"For a painting that no one has seen?" Lucia asked.

"What do you know of a painting?" Corrao asked. "Someone has asked of it?"

"First Benny Carlucco, companion to Don Strachi," Lucia said, "and then Peppone of the newspaper. I had nothing to tell them, I know nothing of it."

Rosina said: "It seems so long ago that Occhi was killed. Do you agree, Giuseppe?"

"Some months, yes. We have hesitated to trouble you, but now it would help to know how anyone came to possess what has been photographed."

"It's been some time since the forms were ordered," Lucia said.

Rosina picked up the photo. "Sister, did we not give Don Cesare a blank order sheet because we had no cards of business?"

"Yes?" Lucia asked.

"You must remember. It was when he asked for a card and you suggested work order to serve as well."

"And you gave it?" Corrao said.

"Yes."

"I cannot recall that," Lucia said, firing a dark eye at Rosina.

Corrao looked to Rosina. "When was that visit, Signorina?"

"In the spring."

"Before Signore Burgundi's disappearance?"

"No, later. I arrived on the day he became missing. I never knew him."

"Have your coffee," Lucia said. "It will be cold."

Corrao poured anisette into his coffee. "Information such as you provide allows further understanding." He sipped the coffee. "Is there anything else?"

"Rosina has told you more than I am able to," Lucia said quickly, avoiding a hardness in Joe's eyes. "If we think of anything that may be important to you, we will call."

She stood; they all stood. Rosina walked the men to the door, and watched them walk off. She returned to Lucia standing at the table, anger in her eyes. "I have become comfortable in this house," she said. "Maybe you have not?"

"It is comfortable here."

Lucia motioned at high ceilings with plaster and oak embellishments, tall windows with curtains and drapes, at teak and cherry wood floors.

"Would you want to lose this to Petrosino and his police?"

"Petrosino would not."

"Giuseppe Petrosino is dead to us," Lucia said. "He is only a policeman and has little place in these fine surroundings."

"He is not dead to me or to your son. He sends gifts to the boy which we accept. He is not dead to your Strachi, whose return you fear, yet find it necessary to keep information from the only man who can keep him away from us."

"Petrosino has not visited us without police purpose."

"Is it not difficult for him to visit a home owned by a Camorrista who saw to the murder of your husband?"

"Again with that?"

"Yes, again with that."

"Did you not hear him say that it was the stableman who killed Enzo?"

"You claim your head is not clear, yet it seems clear to defend Strachi and denounce Petrosino."

"The winds have changed and have made for us a home." Lucia gestured again with her arms, as if to hug the room. "Would you want to lose it?"

"I would be comfortable anywhere," Rosina said.

"But would you choose to lose this?"

"I would not care."

"Then maybe that is why you have spoken too much."

Rosina stepped away. "I must go to the bed."

"Yes, and sleep well with the encouragement you have given the police."

"I will clean the table in the morning."

Lucia's breath quickened. She stepped quickly to end this moment. She placed a hand under Rosina's arm and walked her slowly up the stairs.

"I am unhappy if you are unhappy," she said.

"Don't worry, my sister. I have promised not to leave you."

Rosina turned toward her room and whispered, not meant for Lucia to hear: "If I am unhappy it does not matter."

* * *

Lucia feared losing this house and the security she'd come to cherish, but she feared losing Rosina too. Rosina remained dedicated and available to hold and hug her nephew, quiet his cries, kiss his cheek, his curls and hands and feet, sing as she danced with him in her arms, make him laugh and give so much of the spirit that the two sisters once shared. Lucia had lost her share of spirit, often tried to regain it, but failed, and failed to even cry over it.

In the middle of many nights, she dwelled, as she did now, in the hush of the house, its ticking clocks, a horse clopping by, or a quiet conversation passing by. During these hours, as she traveled the floors, her thoughts sometimes became pleasant. That they would not remain so, that she was suffering as her mother had suffered, she no longer doubted.

Rosina was right. The house belonged to Cesare Strachi and only he could lose it. She had read his first letter, a promise of distant love (that touched her not at all), and passionate embraces upon his return (that touched her with dread).

She had asked Benny on the day he'd delivered that letter: "Is he soon to manage passage back to America?"

"You would know before I did."

"I would know?"

"He would tell you."

"In a letter?"

"Is there another way?"

She'd tossed the letters that followed, still sealed, into drawers around the house, certain that if she did not read of his return, there would be no return, but considered that at some time she must read them and answer them with the same careful words of her note that had manipulated him before.

There had been gifts too, one of them a bracelet of gold and diamonds that she took from the box, then stashed it with some of the letters in some forgotten drawer.

She switched on the light and looked into baby Enzo's room. Except for a scatter of toys and mechanical trains, it had stayed sparse until an American had come some days before.

He needed a shave, smelled of liquor and horses. A cigarette crimped in his lips bounced as he talked. "Delivery for Lucy."

The sisters looked at each other, looked to the man and out the window to his helper and the truck at the curb.

"A crib and drawers and a chair, dolly," the man said. "Kid's stuff."

"We do not want it," Lucia said, as if afraid of it.

"We can't leave without it stays here. Where you want it, dolly?"

The furniture looked nicer now than when the men lugged it up the stairs. But when Benny Bats visited and Rosina showed him to the room, Lucia followed quietly and startled them when she said: "I suppose Don Cesare could not have chosen this furniture. Was it you, Benito? Or one of the others?"

"I know only what Rosina told me," Benny said.

"Oh, I did not know you two enjoy friendship."

But she knew that in good weather, Rosina pushed baby Enzo's carriage down to the neighborhood, an hour away, for breads, cheeses, meats and fish unknown in Madison Square.

During a recent visit, Benny, as if a proud uncle, lifted the baby from the carriage and walked with him into the *Mezzo-*

giorno Social Club. Months old, the kid was a charmer. The guys in the club got to calling him "Sonny," and Sonny charmed the neighborhood with his black curls and shining eyes.

Even the grumpy *calabrese* could not refuse a smile for him, and the *barese* managed singsong praise about the beauty of the boy, his mother and, of course, his aunt. "And tell Lucia we ask after her."

Back home, in the shop, Rosina reported: "The people of our neighborhood ask for you and wish that you are well."

Lucia, pinning a dress pattern, looked up. "I do not need their regards." She motioned to the window at a young family passing by. "The Americans here are as fine as the DiStasis of our home. None talk with bad tongues, and speak only to praise our work."

"And buy little."

"Do you think our people, our own people, would give us even their good wishes? Would they not be envious? Or wear our work to strut and cackle like hens in those dirty streets?"

Rosina said nothing.

"When you speak of the neighborhood, my sister, I no longer think of those people or those streets. I think only that we have made Madison Square our home."

Petrosino Does the Right Thing Again

Lina the Gnome, earrings glistening in the early morning sun, traveled the street as if her feet, hidden under her skirts, never touched the ground. She found Joe, as if he'd been waiting for her, on the steps of Christ the King Church, glancing now and again towards the tailor shop.

No hello, no smile, but an ambush. "Petrosino, as your thick head should now know, the widow has chosen to avoid fear. It is her way. Her future is unfortunate; she will find little peace while in this world. That her mind weakens is both a curse and a blessing for her. You have done your part. Now you must find peace for yourself."

"Good morning, *Piccerella*."

"I am sorry to be urgent. Good morning."

"You are good to come to me with your concern."

"There is a widow, soon to be your wife. With her you will have a child."

"Adelina?"

"Aha, you already know."

"I did not know of a child. That is good. Thank you."

An ambulance stopped at the curb. Joe went to it and took a cane from the driver. He walked off, the cane resting on his shoulder.

Bulldog Joe, who'd made little time for women in his life, had been in and out of gaga for Lucia, and if any good came of women and thunderbolts, they had kicked up feelings of romance and family.

A few women had caught his eye over the years. Adelina Saulino was one of them. Not as pretty as Lucia, but pretty enough. No thunderbolts, but concern and interest for him. Not that he'd forgotten what Rosina had said, that if the dress business were more successful, it would perhaps bring peace to Lucia.

With that, he stepped quickly to Mott Street, passed Chinamen in doorways of hop dens and gambling joints. Where a small woman at a store's street counter sold loose cigarettes, decks of playing cards from France, and sweetened pork rolls, he crossed Mott to the rear of Headquarters and an iron-gated tunnel.

In a basement corridor, with the property room, telegraph office and the sitting room, a cop and his prisoner stepped through a door with a heavy spring that bonged shut on rows of holding cells.

Joe turned into the property room, set the cane on the counter, and got the property cop to laughing.

"Joe, this is the cane you're wanting to trade?" The cop had a brogue. "This thing is from one of the hospitals and couldn't be cheaper."

"So?"

"So? So somebody's gonna catch on, and then what?"

"The case is finished."

"And what will I do when its owner comes for it. Or the DA?"

"No one will come for it. I am to take it to its owner."

"Then sign for it."

"It wasn't my case."

"Then let the owner come for it with a release and he can have it."

"Yes, but you see, the good this will do ..."

"I'd like to help, Joe, but I don't know what the hell you're up to. I don't know."

"The good it will do is more than the trouble that you fear."

The cop folded his arms, looked hard into Joe's eyes. "You're a good dago, a good fella, all right, and I'd like to do it, but ..." He shook his head. "I'll be sorry for this. But you'll please forget about the gun."

"That's the same case."

"What will you bring me to trade, a kid's carpet gun?"

"All right, the cane."

"It's not a cane that you're wanting, Joe," the cop said as he made the trade. "You Eye-talian fellas wouldn't know, but this here is the walking stick of a gentleman. Not a cane, Joe, a walking stick. And a handsome one."

Joe gripped the stick's silver knob with the tips of his fingers. This gentleman's walking stick, like those of western cattlemen, was fashioned from '*i cazz*' of a bull.

* * *

Joe headed for the French Quarter, its streets worse than any street, any alley, any Little Italy. Worse than Minetta Street, with the Africans and Italians ambushing each other; as bad as the African and Irish battles that named a neighborhood San Juan Hill.

The French, or the low of them, hung around basement dives looking dopey and sucking beer with some hocus in it.

Absinthe or something. For the German and Irish cops, *Give me the dagos anytime, then I could tell the good from the bad.*

When Joe was a rookie, they flew the *dago*, the *wop cop*, out of the 13th Precinct up on 30th Street down to the prostitute posts on Mercer and Green Streets.

Joe liked telling war stories about his early years on patrol. Stories that started: "When I had my hair ..." and tales of wine bottles imported from France sailing from roofs and windows that sent him with screeching whores under the cover of fire escapes and into hallways. "Bottles, bricks, rocks. Some of those streets over there, the buildings put you in a box."

Few in the French Quarter liked a cop. The kids did, and the magdalenes did. And the restaurant owners, like Simone with the dancing mammaries that seemed to cheer at the sight of Joe, fed the men on post, kept them around to keep out the stickup men.

Joe never remembered Simone's married name that she dropped after her frog husband, Maurice, got himself collared during Joe's second winter on the job, '84 into '85. Walking the night post on Mercer, Joe sidled into the broken shadow of ashcans and fire escapes to take a leak. He never got to it, because across from him, out of an alley that elbowed to the rear of Simone's restaurant, Maurice crept like a felony in progress, the handle of a bulky valise in his hand and a weighted sack sagged over a shoulder.

Bull Dog Joe locked onto the scent. An easy tail, the street empty and still, Joe hugging the building line, the thick soles of his shoes keeping quiet. On Clinton Street Maurice set down his cargo at the door of a dry goods store and stepped to the side alley of a haberdasher's shop. He needed to pee too.

But Joe was already there, nightstick hanging by its thongs from his badge, finishing his leak and waiting for

Maurice to finish his before snatching him for whatever he was up to.

If Maurice felt life in the dark with him, it took him some seconds to drop his aim, leap into a sprint not as quick as Joe's nightstick, and fall under Joe's boot planted in the small of his back.

Not to roll in weeds and gutter with a guy who'd just peed all over himself, Joe bopped him a few short head whacks with the nightstick — *vaffanculo* — till he stopped squirming. Then he rapped the cobbled street with the nightstick that brought the man from a nearby foot post.

They walked to the station house with the swag — bolts of silks and folds of bed linens — and Maurice, who smelled like overcooked asparagus.

It turned out that the silk got lifted off an East River pier and precinct detectives got interested. They went with Joe to Clinton Street, broke into the store, found its owner and more of the silk, then got the search warrant.

By dawn they'd filled a Black Maria with property, and Joe learned the value of newspapers. Under a photo of the detectives who snatched his stolen-property-felony collar, *The World* said:

> *After a night of investigation at 79 Clinton Street,*
> *Detectives Coffey and Killeen flank the hefty figure*
> *of Marms Mandelbaum, alleged to be the city's most*
> *successful dealer in stolen goods.*

Marms traded three thousand dollars worth of bail for a lam to Toronto. Maurice made his bail and followed her, leaving Simone and her dancing tits jilted and happy with the *Restaurant Du Grand Vatel*, where Joe now headed to meet Benny Bats.

In window reflections he watched himself strut — *'na bella figura* — derby, suit, fresh shirt and collar, and the bull's *cazz'* that he now gripped without scheeving. He turned into the restaurant, its front windows stocked with a half dozen noisy parrots, canaries and cockatoos.

At a table away from the birds, Benny Bats sat with coffee and cognac.

"What's with the circus stick, Joe?" Benny asked.

Joe sat, poured coffee and splashed cognac into it. "Walking stick. You know it?"

"No." Bats put a paper sack on the table. "Sawdust."

"We don't need it, we got it."

"What the hell."

"What the hell? When was the last time you called?"

"They're watching me like a hawk since you nabbed Strachi."

"Getting too successful without the guy you say is your only friend?"

"All right, all right. Come on, have coffee. You're my friend, I know."

Joe set a finger on the sack of sawdust. "When did you get this?"

"Just before."

"Anything interesting?"

"One or two guys at that shit bar. I had a glass of wine that gave me *agita*. I been guzzling *Brioschi*."

"Cognac, coffee and *Brioschi*. Nice. Strachi been in touch?"

"Letters to Carmine Tonno, some for the house uptown that I deliver."

"What's he saying?"

"I don't read the letters, Joe."

"Any word about him getting out?"

"Not that I hear."

"What's Carmine saying?"

"Nothing. He don't like me, but he likes what I bring in. His kid likes me."

"Mootzi?"

"No, fuck him. The other one, Dominic."

"What about him?"

"He's making his father proud. He'll do good."

"Vito San Martino. What's he been doing?"

"Vito Red's up Carmine's ass all time. Carmine's the only guy who likes the little fuck. He's still with the unions, nothing new there, keeps things secret, except when he makes and breaks strikes, and he strong arms membership dues with The Ox."

"Ulino?"

"The Digger. I don't think he knows too much, except to keep his mouth shut. Him and Gaga, fags, I think."

"Anybody talking about the painting?"

"Not that I hear. But Vito visits the fat man."

"Peppone?"

"Yeah."

"What's that mean?"

"There was talk after you guys hit the stable, that the guy who smuggled it in the country was one of the bodies. Was it?"

Joe shrugged. "How do you know what you know?"

"Who else? The Ox. But he don't know more than that, how much it's worth, how they got it ... was supposed to be for the communists, I told you that. So maybe Peppone knows."

"How's that?"

"Vito was an organizer, you know that too."

"Go on."

"And Peppone's a communist too, and they got together."

"When?"

"A few weeks back."

"You said nothing to me about them being together."

"You didn't ask anymore about the painting, I figured it for bullshit."

"The widow. You ask her about the painting?"

"Yeah, I told you right after I asked her. Months ago, when I got a couple of suits. That maybe the tailor had it, but she says no."

"How's their business?"

Benny made a frown, shook his head. "Not good. Carmine got me picking up what they're short for the bills, and Lucia is getting too dopey to know it. Rosina don't like the set up, but she's stuck. She won't leave the sister."

Joe lifted his cup, gulped and poured again.

"A good woman, Rosina — Hey, that cane." Benny tapped the table with a knuckle. "The Marshall's."

"Take it to the dress shop and tell Masterson to pick it up there. Today, do it."

"Okay."

"Tell him to call me after he picks it up."

"But then he knows that we talk, you and me."

"I bet you can dance through that."

Lieutenant Petrosino

Since 1862, when the Police Department moved Headquarters into 300 Mulberry Street, its façade of classic stone got the neighborhood and its cops to calling it the Marble Palace. It was not the department's first Headquarters, but it was the one where the neighborhood went to make a beef, look at lineups and mug shots, or get booked.

From tenements across the street used as news offices, reporters watched, if not for a headline, then for the kids on its stoop tossing jacks or picking-up-sticks. Now that the palace doors stayed shut, kids played on the stoop, but the newspapers moved their offices to buildings around 240 Centre Street, the new Headquarters.

Joe lived a block from the new building, a stone rectangle mounted on a narrow wedge of earth near the north end of the neighborhood. He'd passed there frequently, looking to the top of its four floors, at the windows of the Police Commissioner's office, and at its copper cupola that kids and cops called the rabbi's hat.

The office spanned the width of the building, with windows at each end of it. The view at one end let Commissioner Theodore Bingham see across Centre Street, at beat-up tenements, stores and stables. Windows at the other end looked down on

Centre Market Place, with new gun shops and saloons crammed between tired buildings of lath, plaster and lumber.

The tall Bingham had made a recent problem for himself with an article that quoted him blaming half of the city's crime rate on the Jews. He was way off, had taken hits for it, and laid blame on the Italians by beefing up Joe Petrosino's Squad from six detectives to more than two dozen, titled it the Italian Legion, and promoted Joe to Lieutenant.

"Such a politician," some Jews said.

"Phony bastard," some Italians said.

The orders promoting Joe went citywide on a Thursday, and by dinnertime, the windows of Vincent Saulino's Restaurant steamed with the mix of cold November and the warmth of wine, cooking and celebration.

Detectives watched the new lieutenant at the table where he'd often sat with a meal and a glass of wine, charmed by Adelina, who did not know she'd helped chase Lucia from the warm corners of Joe's mind.

Adelina was thirty-seven, nine years younger than Joe, had already assured him she was eager for babies, and thought it a good time for him to leave the job.

"Twenty-six years is enough."

"Twenty-five," he said, and the next day figured his pension and priced a ring.

❊ ❊ ❊

The doctors had known little of the sickness Mama had suffered, and knew little of Lucia's suffering. Rosina had heard some of the words the doctors threw around, and she asked one to write them for her: *depressive disorder, premature dementia, precocious madness.*

Maybe because it had been too cold and windy to spend time in the sun, Lucia's face had paled, the luster in her eyes had dimmed, and her work in the shop became no more than adequate.

Rosina helped her from the bathtub into her bathrobe.

"Do you think the warm bath brings color to my face?" Lucia asked.

"Yes."

"Did the doctor say it would?"

"Yes, I think so. And now to bed. First Enzo, then you."

Rosina put the baby to bed, kissed him, and smiled because she felt no fever. She stepped into Lucia's room, found her folding down her bedcovers.

"Do you want your slippers, or are you getting in bed now?"

"It feels too early for bed."

"Your slippers then?"

"Yes." Lucia sat on the bed.

Rosina helped her with the slippers and said: "There seems to be no fever."

"Fever?"

"Yes. We thought Enzo was getting sick."

"He is asleep?"

"Yes."

"Oh, no fever, good."

"How do you feel?" Rosina asked.

"All is well."

"Your color is stronger," she said, lying.

"The warm bath brings the color."

"And the men still gaze at you."

"When they come into the shop?"

"Yes."

"I could not go on without you." Lucia said. "But you are tired."

"I will sleep well," Rosina said through half of a yawn. "Are you cold?"

"I am comfortable," Lucia said, holding the bathrobe closed at her neck.

"I have news."

"Yes?"

"Philomena called to me on the street."

"You were with our boy?"

"Yes."

"What does the good Philomena have to say?"

"Petrosino is to be married."

Lucia stood from the bed and stepped behind a wing chair that looked to the fireplace. She smoothed the doily at its top and sat.

"It would be nice to have a fire, to sit again with Cuccio in the kitchen and watch the flames in his eyes. There is wood?"

"This fireplace is gas. I will light it?"

"Yes. I feel chilled now. Will it snow?"

"I have heard no news of snow, but it is cold."

Rosina sparked a flame and Lucia arched her shoulders, capturing the heat of the fire.

"Your back troubles you?" Rosina asked, spreading a blanket on Lucia's lap.

"Giuseppe is to be married? It is certain?"

"There is the date."

Lucia's face smiled, but her eyes did not. "And the bride, do we know her?"

"I think not. She is also a widow."

"Giuseppe seems to favor women he can protect."

"I have thought the same," Rosina said.

"Are there children?"

"No."

"We will make a gift of the gown," Lucia said, and stood as if to begin the gift. "She must come for a fitting and to choose the dress and material. A widow will not want white, but be certain that there is much to choose from."

"The bride is being fitted at this time," Rosina said.

"Oh." Lucia turned her back to the fire. "There will be no invitation. But very well, we will fashion a gown for someone else."

She sat again and lifted her face. "Giuseppe will still watch for us."

"He is no longer dead to us?"

Lucia pulled the blanket to her shoulders. "I suppose I said that?"

"Yes."

"I was frightened to lose our home."

"It is Don Cesare's home. Only he can lose it, and if he does, we will do well elsewhere."

"So you say." Lucia smiled warmly, as if she believed it. "You have gone motoring with Benito?"

"Yes, Sunday."

"The boy smiles to see Benito."

"They like each other."

"Perhaps Benito knows of Don Cesare's return?"

Lucia had asked this question days before, and days before that.

"He has not said," Rosina said.

"Of course not. He said I would know before he did. What is the bride's name?"

"Adelina."

"Adelina is pretty?"

"I have heard, yes."

The house went silent but for the ticking clocks.

Retire or Go to Palermo

Joe Petrosino and Commissioner Bingham sat looking at each other across the walnut width of the commissioner's desk.

"Well, finally Joe, going to Palermo is in the works."

"Go to Palermo?"

"Yes. You forgot? You were part of the idea. Looking through penal records, set up a channel of intelligence, find old informants."

"So long ago we discussed it, and now, when my life has changed ... my child is only months old."

Joe stood slowly and stepped to the window that looked out on Centre Street. He angled his gaze toward Lafayette Street, but could not see the building of his apartment, where he imagined Adelina in the kitchen, singing to the baby and peeking out around the window shade looking for him.

"It was a good idea last year, it will work now," Bingham said. "Your detectives can function for a few months without you."

Joe turned quickly. "Months?"

"Travel to Genoa, Rome, and Palermo. And time, if you wish, to see your home again."

"My home is here." Joe paced across the office to the other

window, this one looking down at cops and detectives un-loading prisoners from a paddy wagon into the Headquarters basement for mug shots and lodging.

He turned to face Bingham. "Adelina and I have discussed my retirement."

"You're still a young man, Joe. What the hell would you do without the job? I trust no one but you to this assignment."

"I am sorry, I must refuse."

An edge came into Bingham's voice. "You would leave the job unfinished?" He leaned forward in his chair. His mous-tache, a pampered handlebar, seemed a weapon.

Joe said: "My family would be happy."

Bingham sat back. "I thought you'd be excited."

"I am excited that you do this, but I ... if I had no family ..."

❊ ❊ ❊

Joe headed down to the squad room. His shoulders sagged with cancelled retirement. He had prepared himself well to leave the job, been to mass almost daily, sorting the dangers and threats through the years that rarely had worried him.

But now, leaving a wife and a child to please Bingham felt as foolish as visiting a city filled with men he had deported, and with families of men he'd sent to the electric chair. He tried to ignore the shaking in his gut. He wrestled with it, finally acknowledged it as fright, and had no idea how to handle it.

"Phone, boss," one of the guys called.

He stepped to his desk and picked up the phone.

"Petrosino."

"Masterson here."

"Yes, Masterson."

"Got a message to phone you."

Joe pictured Bat Masterson in some fancy Tenderloin bar, ladies sashaying, batting painted eyes at the lawman, now known as a gambler, fight promoter and sports reporter for the *Morning Telegraph*.

"Am I having a problem?" he asked.

"There is no problem if you have your walking stick."

"It's good to have it back. Thanks."

"Fine."

"That was a bullshit charge that hillbilly and your guys put on me, you know."

"I know little about it, but I have learned that you are safe from further charges."

"Good to know that. Sounds like there's something you need me to do for you."

"You have met the young ladies of the dress shop?"

"Pretty gals."

"And hard workers. The business is new, and while it is on its way to success, they would not refuse help."

"Help?"

"Perhaps a word in your newspaper."

"I write sports. But I can talk to some of the fancy theater ladies, maybe get them to spend some money."

"A story in your newspaper is not possible?"

"Like I said, I write sports, but I'll talk to people who can."

"That is good of you."

"Did you know that your men took my six gun?"

"Yes, and I have managed to see it. A very handsome revolver."

"The *Colt* people made it special for me."

"I well imagine a strong attachment to a fine sidearm like that, and so I have begun calling for favors owed to me so that I may get it back to you."

"You're a gentleman to do that, Petrosino. Start looking through the *Morning Telegraph,* and you will soon see my appreciation."

❈ ❈ ❈

Joe got to the fourth floor two steps at a time. At his apartment door he smiled to hear Adelina singing. He went in and found her in the kitchen, sitting at the table with the baby in her arms.

"Oh look, Papa's home early," Adelina said, with a smile that took the corny out of love and marriage.

"Not yet, my wife, I have to go back."

He kissed wife and child.

Adelina asked: "Soup I made for tonight, you want?"

"Smells good, but maybe coffee for now, and give me my daughter." He sat at the table and took the baby to his lap.

Adelina at the stove, her back to him, he talked, as if to the baby, of his visit with Bingham.

"... And so, my daughter, because your Papa is so smart, the big boss of the police needs him to go ..."

Adelina turned from the stove, the back of her hand on a hip, the other hand as agitated as her voice. "There is nobody but you in the police? You promised to retire."

"I did not promise, Adelina."

"How do they order you to do this now?" She put cups and the pot of coffee on the table. "I see your face. You are afraid to go."

❈ ❈ ❈

Lina the gnome agreed, and it seemed by chance that as Joe headed back to Headquarters, she found him.

"I will walk with you, Petrosino?"

Joe turned. "*Piccerella*. Yes, come along."

"But slow down, please, we must talk."

They stepped into an easy pace, Lina at Joe's left, then his right as they turned into Grand Street.

"What do you care to talk about?"

"They promise to kill you."

"They have promised for years. You know that. But you protect me, so there is no worry." Joe smiled, as if for a child.

"Your smile is false, Petrosino. You are afraid to go to Palermo."

"If I am to live a long life and die a coward, I will not go. But if I am to do right, I must go."

"Don't go to Garibaldi."

"He will not care to see me."

"Do not joke to what I say, Petrosino. If there is hope for the neighborhood, you must be serious. Lina warns you with reason."

"The neighborhood's passing is no longer certain then?"

"There is always hope and you are the hope."

"I will be safe for you and for the neighborhood."

"You do not dismiss me?"

"I do not dismiss your sincerity."

"And you must believe it."

"I will take care."

Palermo

As the mail boat with Joe Petrosino aboard tied up at Palermo's Piazza Marina, Joe noticed that its sounds and smells differed little from the piers east and west of the neighborhood. He buttoned his coat against February's chill, admiring its light that deepened the colors of sea and sky as did the paintings in Rome that he had visited days before.

A suitcase in each hand, he walked into the marina's square, stopping at the Garibaldi Statue to gaze at the general and pass a few worried thoughts about Lina's warning to not visit him.

Then to the Hotel de France with its dim façade, but a lobby bright and warm. He found his room small and comfortable, with a desk, pen and writing paper.

He wrote to Adelina:

I have today arrived in Palermo. There is much to do and much to see. While in Rome I have seen the Sistine Chapel and Michelangelo's Galleries. Saint Peter's Basilica is beyond human imagination. What a huge, magnificent place! But I am sad to be away and I hope to see my wife and daughter again very soon.

He spent the next days searching through courthouse records, and two weeks of days and nights alone in narrow streets and back roads around Palermo, finding informants who had cooperated with him in the neighborhood, and who would now cooperate in a network of intelligence between Palermo and New York.

He met with Palermo's Police Commissioner Ceola.

"Petrosino," Ceola said, "you travel the most dangerous streets alone. Allow my men to accompany you."

"Thank you, but I have yet to encounter danger and I find cooperation more available when I am alone."

✳ ✳ ✳

Clouds darkened all of Joe's final Friday in Palermo, but not till he returned to the hotel did thunder and lightning drop sheets of rain that chased all activity from the marina.

He tossed his derby on the bed, took off his coat and suit jacket and sat to finish a postcard to Adelina that he had begun earlier that day:

> *A kiss for my wife and for my little girl, who has spent five weeks far from her daddy. Remember me to all our friends and relatives and wish them all a long and healthy life. Another kiss from your affectionate husband.*

He wrote to Charlie Corrao:

> *My Dear Charlie,*
>   *I trust you to do this. The key I handed you will unlock the drawers of my desk. In the right side there is a hand-*

some .45 revolver. It's owner is Bat Masterson of the Morning Telegraph. See that he gets it.

I have made contacts, but with little success. Tonight I must meet with an important person who may bring success.

Affectionately,
Giuseppe

He saw that the rain had lightened, but the piazza remained dark but for the yellow light of gas lamps.

In overcoat and derby, and under his umbrella, he skirted puddles to and around Garibaldi to the Café Oreto, where he'd eaten nearly all his dinners since setting foot in Palermo.

The restaurant was still and quiet, with the bar loud and crowded with men. He sat with his back to the corner at what had become his regular table. Two men walked up to him and remained standing.

"It is arranged, Signore Lieutenant."

"Go. I'll finish and join you."

After Joe

The building was middle-of-the-night quiet as Charlie Corrao climbed the stairs and knocked on the door. Hugging herself in a flannel robe Adelina answered the knock and looked into Charlie's eyes.

"They killed him," she said.

"Yes."

She swooned. Charlie caught her and walked her to a chair in the kitchen.

She reached for a napkin and cried into it. "He was to retire."

"Yes."

She managed words between sobs. "He had a purpose that he had yet to accomplish. To deserve his pension."

"That is what he felt," Charlie said.

"But he was afraid. I know it."

"It is why he went."

She lifted a hand, motioned to her bedroom. "And that baby ... never to know her father. And for what? To show our people as honest and honorable."

Charlie sat across from her. "Yes."

"A boy with a boy's ideas. What is honorable? That they will laugh and celebrate now? What is honest? That he cared less for his wife and his child than for everybody else? There is no honor for me, another husband dead. And for that baby, what is there? A father brave and honorable and dead."

* * *

Rosina woke with the sun angled in her window and the sound of Enzo wanting breakfast. She kicked away her covers and rushed to his crib.

"Good morning, little boy," she said, kissed him and carried him to Lucia's bed.

"I have no milk," Lucia said, her eyes still closed. "Our boy will need the bottle."

Rosina set him on the bed next to his mother. "Then he will have one." She kissed him again and went down the stairs to the kitchen.

She poured milk, cream and honey into a bottle and set the bottle in a pot of water. As it warmed on the stove she stepped to the front door, snatched the newspaper from the stoop and went back to the kitchen.

Standing at the stove she read what American words she could:

LIEUTENANT PETROSINO KILLED IN PALERMO.

The words weakened her, sat her down. She got rid of the first tears and hid the newspaper.

* * *

Philomena Matruzzo found the church filled with sobs and tears, candles and prayers. She hid her anger from Christ, but demanded: "Gesu, if the bad could kill the good Petrosino, who could they not kill?"

At home she talked with the saints about the same thing, then told them that Petrosino, "you must know of him, maybe is confused. Please be with him."

❄ ❄ ❄

Italian Squad detectives opened the envelope sent by Chief Ceola. It held a report and photos of the crime scene. One of the guys prepared a note for his own report:

> *Body, face down, on the ground near the Garibaldi Monument. A fence, iron. Umbrella and derby near Joe. A Belgium revolver in the report (not in any of the photos). Not Joe's gun. His gun in his room, Hotel de France.*
>
> *Shot 4 times. Throat, right cheek, back. Fourth lodged in the material of his overcoat. Newspaper photo of Joe in uniform clipped to the Palermo report. Found on the ground.*

❄ ❄ ❄

It had been unreasonable, Lina admitted. Fate could not allow mercy. It didn't know how; she didn't know how. Fate and she had little to do with rights and wrongs.

She'd known that she was fate, or at least a representative of fate, an observer. But the tears, the few that had dampened her eyes, puzzled her. She had suspected her purpose in the neighborhood was to help deliver it gently through the final pages of its life. She had comforted many, she had cured fears and ills. But it seemed insignificant now.

Joe Petrosino, the sturdy hope of the neighborhood, had been destroyed. She could do little to ease the pains of his death, she had not saved him, and so she could not save the neighborhood.

Others would try, she knew, but that was all the books said about it.

Reciprocation

The United States Secret Service had triggered the run for the Morellos months back, but the neighborhood figured that Clutch Hand Morello's 30-year sentence for making and moving funny money sent a salute to Joe.

The Squad didn't say otherwise, but as soon as Adelina buried her husband in Brooklyn and moved near the cemetery, they started hitting Mafia and Camorra spots in Brooklyn, Harlem and the neighborhood. They attacked like warriors. They broke up furniture, ripped out phones, clogged the Tombs and the courts with misdemeanors beefed up to felonies, and never considered the usual courtesy that let betting receipts and records alone.

Morello sent out word for one of his brothers to take over the crew, but bosses in New Orleans and Palermo had not okayed the growing counterfeiting caper, got no pieces of it, got nothing but heat, and gave the operation of the old crew to the businessman and level headed soldier, Pasquale Patsy Stellato, brother of Happy Carmine's roly-poly wife.

* * *

Benny Bats drove Happy Carmine up to the Bronx, to the gravel driveway of the Pelham Heath Inn, a party place where the Bronx and Pelham Parkway cut past farms around the Eastchester Road.

Patsy Stellato, flowing black moustache on a round, sad face, didn't smoke, didn't drink. He was seated at a table with two guys and a pot of coffee. When Carmine and Benny walked in, the two guys left, Benny with them, and left Stellato with Carmine and the pot of coffee.

"This peace we had, all of us doing good," Patsy said right off. "No?"

"Yeah."

"But with all this shit going on," Stellato said, looking hard at Carmine, "it's making bad feelings, we're all losing."

Carmine nodded.

"You wasted no time getting your friend out of that fucking prison to do this?"

"None of us got him out," Carmine said. "We didn't know about it. Any okay he got, he got over there."

"And him. He didn't know what would happen? Goes there like the peasant that he is. This is business, not cowboys and Indians. You been running things, keeping things good, peaceful. And I'm trying to keep peace too, Carmine, do things with all the crews. Bronx, Brooklyn, Harlem. People losing money, cops wrecking our joints, people scared to even put a few pennies on a number. They know we're sitting down, me and you, and they wanna hear what they wanna hear."

"Whatever we gotta do," Carmine said.

"The cops want who killed one of their own. I don't blame them. You blame them?"

"No."

"Then do the right thing."

* * *

Raining now, Benny drove under the Third Avenue "L".

Crossing 116th Street, Carmine pointed. "We got a couple of spots over there, Pleasant Avenue. You know them, you made them, you and Georgie Nuts." He pointed with his chin. "Some of the market we got. The rest is Mo Zito's. Good things came from Joe Morello and Patsy Stellato sitting down with Strachi and me. We did okay back then. It was that or a war, and Zito's been good with it. Years now we been living rich. But now the cops killed all his spots."

"Where is he? Strachi."

"Upstate. With the cows, the milk. He thinks we're getting things in order before he gets back."

"They not gonna do it up there?"

"No. Don't you understand? It's ours."

Benny, the guy who wanted nothing to do with breaking heads and busting knees, knew he'd have no problem putting one or two in Strachi's head. Do it for reputation, yeah, but for Joe Petrosino too. All those times he called Joe his only friend, words that fell out of his mouth like yak — if it was yak then, it was honest-to-God now. When he got the word that Joe got hit, it felt no different than when they told him about his father frozen and dead under the snow.

❊ ❊ ❊

The rain had left the neighborhood, let a warm breeze dry the streets and let the sun angle through the stained glass of the *Patarama Holy Family Chapel.*

"He's giving it to Dominic," Benny told The Ox.

"Why him?"

"To get him a button. What else?"

"How you figure that? He ain't a siggie."

"His mother is."

"But Carmine ain't."

"He does this, see what happens. This is America, things are loose."

"Rules don't matter no more?"

"Not for this. That's why you're driving."

"Me? If he wanted me in this, I woulda went to the meet up the Bronx with him. Something's going on."

"Maybe he's trying you."

"How about he tries you? You went with him up there."

"He don't want me."

"Don Strachi's good to me."

"If you don't do it, you gotta scram," Benny said.

"Where the hell am I gonna scram?"

* * *

Then came the day the newspapers wrote about. The temperature dropped from warm to cold. The sky went gray, more like black. The street lights snapped on. The wind, forget about it. Sheets of plywood, doors and bundles of lathe from the top floors of construction sites sailed over Brooklyn and Manhattan and landed in Staten Island with laundry, horse blankets and plate glass.

Lightning blasted a smokestack in Brooklyn and flattened it in a brewery's engine room, killed a guy. Two horses pulling a truck got zapped and they dropped.

Up near City Island fishing boats disappeared. In Washington Heights wind pulled a baby from its mother's arms. In Harlem it ripped up a circus tent, tangled people in canvas and dropped a tent pole that cracked a little girl's skull.

Subways got flooded. The bottom acres of the Central

Park got to looking like swamp. Limbs snapped off trees, people ran into the Arsenal Station, or got herded by the floods to overpasses that arched above the water line.

A milk wagon nearly stalled, then bucked out of the park onto Fifth Avenue. A tree crashed down behind it and blocked 72nd Street. Dominic Tonno, The Ox, and the wagon rattled south.

"It stays dark, we don't wait till tonight?" The Ox asked.

"Let's see if we get through this shit."

They zigzagged around stalled autos, trolley cars and downed wires. On the Bowery they moved under the "L", creeping past storefronts lighted for night, turned into Broome Street, crossed Centre Street and Police Headquarters.

"What you think?" The Ox asked.

"Go around the front."

They stopped where steps led into the new palace, left the wagon there. It sat a few hours before somebody looked inside. Then the phone call to the Italian Squad sent Detectives Charlie Corrao and Ugo Casadei to look into the wagon, smell rancid milk, and see the body of Don Cesare Strachi with a garrotte around most of his neck; and a scrap of paper pinned to the lapel of his suit: *For Petrosino.*

The body got to the morgue, Corrao and Casadei got to Mott Street for chicken with black bean sauce. After the fortune cookie, Casadei asked: "How we closing this one out?"

"The way Joe would close it out."

The homicide stayed open and ignored.

❋ ❋ ❋

The Digger watched the barber shave Strachi, give him a haircut, and helped put him in a suit. Then, in the coffin storage room with Vito Red, The Digger put his hand on a casket. "This one."

Vito pointed to another. "That one is finer."

"Okay, that one," The Digger said.

Vito, a steady earner with the unions, jobs and strikes, had wormed himself into the money end of the funeral business, Benny saying he climbed up Carmine's ass like cheap underwear. The Ox saw that too, and everybody saw that the scrawny man had gotten scrawnier. His eyes got bigger and his pants got baggy. Sick over the guy in the coffin, maybe, but if he got to looking like a weed, it came after the fire of the Triangle Shirtwaist Factory.

One-hundred-fifty girls, many from the first picket line he had broke, either burned, suffocated, or flew ten stories to the street and into pine boxes lined up on the North River pier at 26th Street.

Sick or not, Vito stayed the mercenary, sending strike breaker muscle to the pier, but to move slowly and softly through the lines of boxes, hustling Patarama compassion for families looking for what was left of wives and daughters.

Parades of hearses slunk back and forth from the funeral home to the pier, to the morgue, and to Gaga and The Digger. Traffic around Patarama got thick. The preparation room stayed up for most of a week, embalming machines clicked and hummed and, with cash overflowing the till, Carmine threw a salute to Vito, the reason for the overflow, and tossed him a key to the till.

Few knew about that till, a locked box bolted to a closet floor in the Patarama office. The Digger knew, Gaga didn't. He just knew he got whatever The Digger gave him as long as he did what he was told.

Never had he failed to respect or pleasure The Digger. Mister Ulino, to him. But lately the boy's face took on looks The Digger had never seen on it. Looks that made jealousy and worry, the way it grinned at the young ladies who came to mourn; the way he hummed to the girls whose hair he combed and cheeks he colored to look pretty in their coffins.

In the middle of a night, their bedroom dark but for the glow of street lamps outside, Gaga had been studying shadows slide along the walls and ceiling. He stayed quiet till The Digger stirred.

"Did you see, Mr. Ulino, that Mr. Strachi had no hair in his ears?"

"You put a little too much color in his face."

"I'll fix it now?"

"No, go to sleep now. He's gone in the morning anyway. I just want you to notice. Women like a little more color, but not men."

"Yeah, women. Pretty women," he said. "Right, Mister Ulino?"

The Digger said nothing.

Gaga said: "I like to see them with no clothes and I like to dress them too, but I like the alive ones when I make believe they have no clothes on. I would like to touch them like I touch the others."

"Touch the dead ones. The alive ones are not for you. You will be in trouble with the police if you touch them and I will miss you when you are in jail."

With a tone The Digger had never heard come from him, Gaga said: "You will be in trouble with the police if they knew what we do."

"What we do in love is our secret," The Digger said, tugging an end of his moustache at a corner of his grin. "You know that. And it is not wrong for us."

"I want to love a pretty girl like the one in the back parlor."

"You don't hear? What did I just tell you?"

"I don't care, I want to love one."

"You don't love me?

"I don't want to do that anymore."

"I will give you money. So much money that you can leave here whenever you want and find live girls."

"Where would I go?"

"A stable with horses. One with rabbits."

"Okay, I'll love you again if you give me money."

"Meet me downstairs."

"Why not here, Mister Ulino?"

"Downstairs. Go and wait for me."

The Digger found Gaga in the stock room, lying curled in the coffin they had used many times. He was sucking his thumb. The Digger backed off when tears got behind his eyes, but he regained, used chloroform, then held the coffin pillow to Gaga's face.

The flimsy corpse fit neatly under the blanket of the girl in the back parlor. By noon, after a mass had been said for them, they were buried.

❋ ❋ ❋

After a day of burials, The Digger walked the alley to the *Mezzogiorno* cellar, found nobody there, then went upstairs. Out front, beyond San Gennaro, he saw Benny Bats and the little boy, the son of Lucia Burgundi, talking with Vito Red.

He caught Vito's eye, then waited for him in the kitchen.

"You have the money?" The Digger whispered.

"What money?"

"From the drawer. It is empty."

"Did you look — "

"I looked all over."

"How much was it?"

"You counted last."

"Where's Gaga?"

"I have not seen him since yesterday."

"The drawer was locked?"

"Of course it was. My keys are gone too."

Gaga stayed gone and suspicions hung on. But both faded to history as the Patarama books went real black. Vito had parlayed the Triangle tragedy with Mafia and Camorra compassion and grief. Patarama funerals buried Sicilians, Neapolitans, Calabrians, and grudges that came from across the sea with them. It made for new alliances, new money, and succeeded at a pace toward what would come to be known as the Mafia-Camorra peace.

❋ ❋ ❋

Rosina found success too. For the business and for the troubled Lucia. She felt it coming each time ladies of Madison Square turned into the Twenty-fourth Street to look beyond the fence of iron pickets at the shop signed *LuciaRosina*.

Now and then, one or two of the ladies came into the shop, fingered fabrics and *oohed and aahed*, studied sketches and *oohed and aahed*. But their visits resulted in polite conversation and limited fittings.

Then, on a Thursday in December, at the start of a snow, Rosina watched Benny leave Georgie Nuts in the car, quick step into the shop and toss packs of peanuts on their work table.

"Ladies, it will be a good Christmas. I promise."

"For what, Benito?" Rosina asked, smiling at the promise, whisking snow from Benny's shoulders. "For the peanuts?"

"More than peanuts, Beautiful," he said, and yanked *The*

Morning Telegraph from inside his coat. "Because of Louella Parsons."

"Who is that?"

"She writes in this paper." Benny slapped the folded newspaper with the backs of his fingers. "About actors and singers, moving pictures. And now you."

He put a finger on the Parsons column and read:

> *LuciaRosina, a shop of elegance run by two talented and lovely sisters of Italy, has been gaining attention from the ladies of the stage. Good rumor has it that the Floradoras have been fitted for the sisters' Milano inspired fashions.*

Benny ran a finger down the column. "And here she says she comes here herself."

"Nobody come here," Rosina said. "No Louella, no nobody."

"What is the Floradoras?" Lucia asked. "Cigars, no?"

"No. The Floradoras are girls that sing and dance in the theaters. Everybody knows them. Show girls."

"No Floradora," Rosina said. "Something is a mistake."

"No, no, no," Benny said. "If Louella Parsons says they come here, they come here."

A group of ladies, their eyes wide with anticipation walked in.

"Aha," Rosina said.

Prohibitions

That year and years after, the dress shop profits grew. So did Benny's thoughts for Rosina. His first sight of her so long ago — those gray eyes, true and sincere, smart and innocent — had sent him into hot and cold shivers that she must have felt when she measured him for his first suit with her. He'd sensed she feared him then, or just didn't like him.

But then came the Sunday drives, lunches, dinners, and picnics up in City Island, or down at the Battery. It was in the Central Park, during a walk that should have been shorter, that his limp got to showing itself.

"I think you are sometimes in pain?" Rosina asked.

"A little, yeah, but it's nothing."

"You do not like that I ask?"

"No, it's okay."

"It is no shame to have pain."

"Marry me."

"No."

The soft spot in his heart for Rosina — most called her Rose by now, Benny stuck with Rosina — tried to toughen, but it stayed mushy. No jealousy from her, no demanding, no whining, but a pain in the ass with the kid, Sonny, all the time. Being with her meant being with him. Out to Jersey, down to

Coney Island, a boat around Manhattan and, finally, a Sunday
in the Bronx and a building lot on the Williams Bridge Road.

They left the kid sleeping in the car and kept eyes on the
car as they stepped into a wooded parcel on ground spongy
with melting winter.

Benny said: "Rosina, look. Over here could be the kitchen,
or it could be the dining room. The guy's doing the plans." He
stepped close to her, his eyes locked on hers. "The house could
look this way so the kitchen would get the sun in the morning.
Unless you want it looking that way, whatever you want."

"But, Benito —"

"I'm talking a house for you, Rosina."

"We have a house, Benito."

"That's Strachi's house."

"Lucia says it will be hers."

"Don't make book on it."

"What?"

"Never mind. But this house will be yours. All you gotta
do is ... here, look."

He took a ring box from his pocket, opened it. "White
gold, like what my father got for my mother. But the guy says
he could put the diamond, three carats, he says it is, in regular gold if you like. Or change the stone. The trains are coming
up this way. The house will be worth ... forget about it."

She let him slide the ring on her finger and let him lock
her hands in his. She let go a tear and an embrace, and set a
cheek on his shoulder.

"You have so many women, Benito."

"But not the woman I want."

"And once you have her?"

"I'm talking a wedding, Rosina."

"Oh, Benito ... my obligations ..." She looked to the car. "It
is impossible."

Benny said: "The boy has a mother."

"His mother and I are one now," Rosina said. "Lucia cannot be alone, her life is my life."

"The ring promises your future to brighten."

"The future is written." She pushed herself from his shoulder and handed him the ring.

The gold felt warm in his palm. Angered, he turned to walk away, but stopped and faced her.

"You will wear it some day."

"By then I will be fat and you will not care to have me."

"Not fat. Chubby. And still I'd want you. How could I not want you, with that face so — "

"Oh, look, the boy is awake. He will be frightened," she said, and scrambled quickly to the car.

Forget about it.

PART TWO

The Problem

Forget about it. How many times he must have said that since before Prohibition and the years into it. He still had the ring and the problem, the problem pretty much a man now, knocking on the door to the cellar office of the *Mezzogiorno*.

"Come in."

"You wanna see me?"

"Yeah."

Sonny came in, stood near the door. His black curls were not combed, they didn't have to be. His clothes, probably measured, tailored and cut by his Aunt Rose, fit him well. The punk looked sharp.

Benny took a paper sack from a desk drawer, put it on the desk.

"I was gonna ask you something anyway," Sonny said.

"What?"

Sonny stepped to the desk. "Me and Mootzi, we been thinking about a spot. A speak."

"Think about this." Benny tossed him the sack.

Sonny caught it, held it like he knew what it was. "What?"

"Look at it."

Sonny opened the bag, dumped a diamond broach and a hundred dollar bill on the desk.

"Her mother came to me with this," Benny said.

"Yeah, so?"

"Crying, she comes to me, because everybody connects me to a misery like you."

Sonny shrugged, made a face like *I don't care.* "Come on, you cuzzy with my aunt, everybody does things."

Benny percolated real fast, wound up the punch before he bolted out of the chair, hammered Sonny on the chin, grabbed a handful of shirt and a handful of curls, shoved him against the concrete wall, and connected a few more punches.

"You got nothing to say about your aunt. You understand me?"

"All right, all right, I'm sorry. All right."

Benny let go, Sonny felt his face for blood, found some at his nose.

"How she went with you, this kid, I don't know. You sure ain't Valentino. Then you give her a hundred to get rid of it? Get a fucking abortion, cocksucker?"

"Let me get my handkerchief. I'm fucking bleeding."

"And a cheap fucking diamond to keep her quiet? You're some fucking prize."

Benny let go, fixed his tie, sat half his ass on the desk.

"You know why the mother came to me?"

Sonny shrugged, eyes black and wide behind the handkerchief at his nose.

Benny stood again. "Because she goes to her husband, he rips your face off. I told her I can't keep this from him. She says wait, that maybe things could get better. Then she tells me the kid loves you. Loves a fucking hobo like you."

"She said she'd stay quiet," Sonny said.

"Yeah, well, she didn't. Look, I can't go to bat for you. Better get some scram money together. Or get a good diamond. What's her name?"

"Who?"

"Who. Who we talking about, you fucking jerk?"

"Antoinette."

"Antoinette a dog?"

"She ain't a dog."

"Marry her."

"You serious?"

"The ring, candy, flowers, all that shit."

"A wife?"

"If the father lets her marry you. Maybe you'll get your speak then, or maybe he'll do a favor and put you in a barrel."

"A fucking kid you want me to have."

"And pray he ain't a jerk off like you. Now go do what you gotta do and don't come back if you don't."

* * *

Sonny seesawed between lamming and setting up house, then he hooked up with Mootzi, Happy Carmine's nutsy kid, and Carmine got them near being legit running truckloads of factory whiskey out of Canada down to the Bronx for some guy they didn't know and couldn't get to know. They delivered a few loads, made a few scores, till Mootzi grew himself a brainchild.

He had a way about him. A hard head and an iron look in his eyes that challenged, or threatened, or did something that kept Sonny from thinking for himself.

"Look at all this money these guys are making with what me and you are moving for them, breaking our ass," Mootzi said. "Money we'll never make if we don't get *cugliones*. So I say fuck these guys, and we make some moves, you and me."

They were hours out of Canada, hauling cases of Canadian Club.

"Moves like what?" Sonny asked.

"You just relax and you'll see. Go to sleep."

Hours later Mootzi drove past the delivery spot in the Bronx.

"Where you going?"

"Did I tell you to relax?"

Mootzi drove to a garage on Park Avenue. Cold like that, no deal, no invite. He says they'll make bones with Dutch Schultz, and if they screw the guy who owned the truckload, Dutch would make it okay and they would start shoveling in some real money.

"Are you fucking kidding?" Sonny said.

"No *cugliones*, no gelt."

"I don't know, man."

Mootzi parked the truck in the garage's driveway. "Go knock."

"You go knock."

"Come on, get balls."

"It's five in the morning, Mootzi. What if somebody's sleeping in there?"

"So wake them up. What the fuck is it with you? Go knock."

Sonny knocked on the door next to the overhead. A guy with the face of a fist opened up. "What is it?"

"We got something maybe you wanna see."

"What is it?"

"Canadian."

The guy looked at the truck. "Who you with?"

"Mo Zito."

"Zito hears you say that, he kills you."

"Maybe we got the wrong place."

"You fucking guineas."

Next day Benny caught the beef. *These two kids, Benny. One of them is Carmine's, the other one's yours. They used Mo's name. Carmine says for you to handle it.*

* * *

Soaping up his face at the bathroom sink, Benny got tickled that maybe the two jerks drove themselves into forever. Carmine Tonno would be better off without this son. Patsy Stellato's daughter, Antoinette, and the baby in her belly would do better without Sonny Burgundi. But knowing Patsy, he'd give Antoinette whatever she wanted, and knowing Sonny, he'd take all he could.

Benny shaved and toweled his face and stayed at the mirror. Forty-five years looked back at him. Choppers still pearly, eye pouches just coming on, black hair dappled with white, same with the moustache.

On the handle end of the rake, an apartment up in midtown — same building where actor George Raft lived and partied with guys from Harlem — closets and drawers crowded with clothes. A new car once in a while, the newest one a Lincoln with eight cylinders and Georgie Nuts steady at the wheel.

The connection with Georgie and Benny had been remade by Dominic Tonno. Smart and careful like his father — and nothing like his wacky brother — he kept markers on all his crew (the bigger the earner, the bigger the marker), and kept them knowing only what they needed to know.

Patsy Stellato had put Happy Carmine on the speakeasies operation, with the okay to give it to Dominic. Buying and selling boot couldn't keep too many secrets, but it made a lot of whispers.

Dominic sent guys upstate to rent and buy houses and storefronts for cooking bootleg. They picked spots for the speakeasies, garages for cars and trucks, guns, ammo, cash. Truces and heads got broke, fixed, broke.

Stellato got to running the family the way things got run in

Sicily: Boss, Consigliere, Capos and Soldiers. He kept his family small. That was his way, the trusted and familiar. Like with Happy Carmine, who he couldn't call Consigliere because he wasn't Sicilian. But Consigliere was what he'd made of himself since the good things that came out of the Camorra-Mafia sit-downs.

Then Dominic got made. A lot of talk, envy and jealousy, but no surprise.

He ain't a Siggie, so what. He's Happy Carmine's son, he's Patsy Stellato's nephew.

Carmine had been keeping the kid's head low, waiting for the right time, and the right time came when he'd whacked Strachi and got himself a button. Nobody disapproved. Nobody ignored The Ox either, recognized him and feared him, but none of Strachi's old Camorra crew got made. Then, who's made, who's not made, nobody kept count as long as barrels of booze got poured into barrels of cash.

The enterprise filled the neighborhood with cash it never had before. Buying and selling real estate got expensive, but if you could sleep through sirens and shots fired in the middle of nights, it made for a solid place to live.

* * *

Benny got dressed, called Georgie Nuts.

"Hello."

"Yeah, George. Me. Listen. That call I got about the Bronx beef?"

"Yeah."

"Find out where Nicky Coco is and come get me."

Philomena Matruzzo Four

By now the bank book under Philomena's bed counted up to nearly one hundred dollars, and the hatbox got crowded with Laurio's certificates of Birth and Baptism, First Communion and Confirmation, and photos of Laurio with other boys, acolytes to Don Camillo. His graduation certificates were in there with a studio photo of him, broad shouldered and handsome, in a white shirt and a tie hand-tinted red by the photographer.

Mother and son had learned the language of America together, and together they spoke it. Laurio barely had an accent.

"I need to keep some money from my pay this week," he said.

His pay came from Armando Peppone and *Mondo Nuovo*.

"For why you need?"

"I need a shirt."

"And for why you need a shirt?"

"A special shirt, Ma. Black one."

She asked no more questions. The years of novenas and talks with the saints were paying off. Laurio had said nothing further, and to keep the evil eye from hearing about it, neither did she.

Days after he brought home the shirt, a hot Friday afternoon, she'd been preparing Don Camillo's dinner, and she had Laurio, just home from work, try on what she still called the priest's jacket.

"Ma, again?" Laurio said. "It's too short. What do you think, it grows?"

"Maybe I fix."

He put it on. She smoothed the material at his shoulders, tugged on the sleeves and lifted the cuffs to see if any length had been sewn under. "Good, maybe take out," she said.

She tugged on the hem at the back of the jacket and, folding it up to see the lining, said: "Yeah, maybe I fix. From where you come I no know. You Papa short like me."

"You cook the good foods and I grow like the Americans. In *Italia*, they gonna grow long too."

"Why they gonna grow?"

"Mussolini."

"Go away, Mussolini."

"Mussolini is good for Italy." Laurio took off his tie. "And for us here too."

Used to be that Philomena rarely heard mentions of Benito Mussolini without someone making a face. But talk had changed. His pictures filled American newspapers with those eyes like Vito Red's eyes and that sour mouth.

"One minute," she said. "For why you have the black shirt?"

"Because that's what I am. A Blackshirt." He said it as if to please her.

"And you no tell me."

"I just told you."

"How stupid I am."

"Stupid? What?"

"No for be a priest?"

"It is more important to be with Mussolini. Together we will make these Americans afraid to call us names."

"Who? You and him?"

He stuck out his chest, squared his shoulders and distorted his mouth into a look of Mussolini that made Philomena turn away.

"Nobody want Mussolini," she said with a short scream.

"Even the Pope says he was sent by God, Ma."

"Look, no black shirt, please. See how nice you look with the white shirt."

She took his hand and examined the white shirt's sleeves. Since first working for Peppone, printer's ink kept the cuffs stained.

She had asked: "It is clean at the newspaper?"

"Sure. I clean it."

"Why the shirt gets like this?" Gripping his arm, she showed him a cuff. "I no can wash."

"The ink, Ma. From the press. I'll take it to the Chinks."

"No Chinks. Roll up the cuffs, keep from the ink."

"I'll buy another shirt."

"Just like that you spend money?"

He took his mother's hand from his arm and kissed it, then took off the white shirt, hooked it on a finger and held it before him.

"This shirt, Mama, is for work," he said, and tossed it at the sink. He took the black shirt from the hook near the bedroom door. "And this one is for you and me and Italia."

"Italia no care for you and me. And tie you shoe or you fall."

Laurio sat to tie his shoe and Philomena poked his head with a knuckle. "Peppone finds what's in this head of yours ..." She tugged at his curls.

"Ouch. Come on, Ma."

"… He take job from you."

"*Il Duce* says Italians will make our own jobs, even in America. Peppone and his Russians can't promise that."

"Never mind *Duce* and the Russians. They for other people. You work, save money, and take care for yourself."

Laurio stood and put on the black shirt. "Okay, I'm going."

"Where you go?"

"A meeting."

"You no look like my son with that shirt."

"I'm your son, Ma. I'll see you later."

"Wait. The fish for Don Camillo. You bring."

"I'm late. See you later." He opened the door, stepped out.

Never before had Laurio's footsteps sounded like the footsteps of his father, those years ago, falling fast and faster down the stairs. But when her husband had gone to dig silver in the west, she locked the door behind him, then scrubbed the pans that had made his breakfast, scoured the sink, and never cried for him.

Now, with the footsteps of her son too distant to hear, she didn't lock the door and didn't scrub, but the door latched itself and she let go the tears behind her eyes. Sobbing into her apron, she paced, asking the saints what she'd done wrong. She felt no reply and, angered at their betrayal, shut her lips to lock in the curses running through her head and held the black jacket, first to her breast, then onto the kitchen table.

She sat, slid her glasses to the tip of her nose, scissored the stitching in the cuffs, and measured a new length. About to do the same with the hem at the back of the jacket, she found a repair had already been done. Perhaps work that the tailor did for the priest those years past.

Then, feeling something — a flat irregularity, maybe a patch, a wrinkle or a fold in the material. She opened the hem's stitching, put her hand under the lining and took out a purse of a fine black silk that recalled her dreams of gems and gold.

Her breathing pitched, she removed the purse, kneaded it, felt something, but not gems and not gold. She stood, her knees soft. She checked the door locks, rushed Saint Anthony from the bedroom — *you see this too* — lit fresh candles before him and Rocco, then sat at the table and fixed herself in the moment.

She shuffled to the edge of the chair. Carefully, quietly, as if someone could hear, she opened the purse and removed a painted canvas about the size of Laurio's handkerchiefs. She set the canvas flat, then angled it to better see a skinny man, with features sad and grotesque, sitting at a table with a meal of poor people before him. She tilted the canvas this way and that to find treasure, but found only disappointment.

But not in the saints, not in the dreams, and not in the painting, only in herself, too dull to recognize meaning. But, she concluded with satisfaction, that what she could not recognize now, would make itself known, if not to her, then to Laurio. If not now, then in time.

Her breathing eased, the sad man back in the purse, she put him in a paper sack and dropped the sack into the important hatbox. Then she removed Peppone's article about lost art being returned by a good and honorable man. She read it again, put it back and slid the hatbox under the bed.

"Keep an eye on it," she told the saints.

Back in the kitchen she put Don Camillo's dinner in a shopping bag, folded the jacket over her arm, and began the walk to the *Mondo Nuovo* storefront window.

She had passed here many times, looked beyond its gold and red letters to Laurio sweeping the floor, cleaning the press, or inspecting the tabloid sheets that the press coughed into stacks. She slowed now to see more carefully the worn surfaces of the machinery and the alphabet clumped in bins of a shallow wood tray. In a corner at the rear, a desk sat angled, a telephone and a typewriter on it with scatters of paper fluttering under a ceiling fan.

Behind the desk, a beat-up easy chair held Peppone, his girth, all his chins and his waxed mustache, and the same stained collar and white flannel he wore in all weather. Philomena did not like the man, but for more than a year he'd paid Laurio a fair and steady salary. She managed a smile and walked through the door.

Peppone stood, wiped sweat from his face with a handkerchief that had been at his neck. "Signora Matruzzo, it is good to see you." He made a show of closing the top buttons of his shirt, fixing his collar. "So many times I see you pass. May I get a drink for you?"

"No, nothing, thank you."

Peppone motioned to a kitchen chair facing the desk. "Please sit and tell me what I may do for you."

She took the jacket from her arm, hung it on the back of the chair, sat and looked to the doughy face of the man.

"Tell me, Signore Peppone, Laurio is doing his job so that you are pleased?"

The question seemed to surprise Peppone. "He does well."

"He is polite, he listens to what you say?"

"He is a good boy. If he is not happy ..."

"No, no. I am a mother checking on her son."

The talk had turned into a mix of American and *napulitan'*. "He is done for the day, you must know."

"Yes, I know," Philomena said, lifted a sleeve of the jacket and brushed it with her fingers.

"This jacket must be Don Camillo's," said Peppone. "You have done work for him?"

"No work and no his jacket."

A new look came over Peppone. His lips fell open and his eyes wandered. He leaned back, then forward, and asked: "How long have you had it?"

"The wife of the tailor, you remember?"

"Yes. Poor thing is not well, I hear."

"Not well, no."

"Then you have had the coat for some time since she gave it to you."

"She no give. It stay when she go, and I keep because maybe the priest gonna come."

"Priest?"

"A priest, yes. You don't know?"

"I know of a Sardinian, who said he was a priest, but was not."

"Why you say he no priest?"

"Many whispers come to me, Signora."

"Where he is now?"

"Some say he was a thief and ran off, others say he was killed for the value of art that he had."

"Art like a picture?"

"A painting. Of a blind man."

"Blind. Poor thing. You see him?"

Peppone's round face got long for a moment. "Perhaps you know something more of this story?"

"What could I know?"

"Something someone may have said?"

"Nobody say. Ask the one who told you."

Peppone sat back, folded his hands at his chest. "The painting has become more valuable now than when this jacket came to the neighborhood."

"And one is something for the other?"

"Signora, you must go to no one with the painting."

"What you say? I no have painting."

"But the artist has made a larger version and it has become famous. There will be much money for someone who has the first one."

"Why much money?"

"You have heard of the artist? The Spaniard, Picasso?"

* * *

Philomena blessed herself with the church's holy water, then walked on a side aisle to the rectory office, where Don Camillo sat in a cushioned chair, his curls short, but looking like the cherub curls of Church paintings, and his eyes soft and almost black. He would greet her, she knew, after reading from the small book that he read every day.

She stepped through to the kitchen, hung the jacket on a coat rack, and set the priest's dinner, cool by now, on the stove to warm. She sat, wove rosary beads through her fingers and reached the second decade when Don Camillo came to the table.

"Good evening," he said.

She stayed seated. "Good evening, Don Camillo."

"So hot to cook, but I smell fish?"

"Yes, with the rice. But no good evening."

"Why no good?"

"Laurio wears a black shirt. Not for a priest, but for Mussolini. Do you know of this?"

"No."

"I have prayed that he be a priest, but as the Son of the Virgin — that poor woman — sheds His blood, my ungrateful son betrays them for gangsters with souls blacker than their shirts."

She stood, scooped the dinner onto a plate and set it before Don Camillo. "So many prayers I have offered, and the saints have betrayed me."

"No, no. We have yet to know what they have done."

Philomena opened her mouth to speak, but the face of the man in the painting came to her and stopped her. She needed to see him again.

"I bring for you this jacket," she said, motioning to the coat rack. "See if you like. I must hurry."

❀ ❀ ❀

Twilight softened the colors of sunset as Philomena resumed the rosary on her walk home. The shoemaker, leaving his shop, tipped his hat to her. The bread store, dark and vacant, reminded her that the baker was sick, and she would mention him to the saints.

She continued the rosary as she hurried up to her flat. She switched on the lamp on her dresser, took the painting from the hatbox and set it in the lamp's glow. She moved Saint Anthony to let him see what she had not seen until the face of the man came to her at Don Camillo's table.

"Look, Anthony. You see he is blind? See? He is the treasure."

Philomena apologized to the saints for her anger and for accusing them as unreliable. She wondered with them what to do with the painting. Give it to Don Camillo and let him worry about it? Keep it till the day of Laurio's vows?

She stepped lively into the kitchen humming songs about the sun, sky and sea she'd thought forgotten. She felt gratitude for the saints, a greater nearness to them, and a thought came to her.

"Do you suppose that after he takes his vows you will see that he is sent to our church here? Anthony, Rocco? Anybody? Yes, I know, you have done much already. Please be patient with me."

She filled the sink with hot water, dropped in a bar of brown soap and a washboard, set her feet firmly on the floor and, as she ended the rosary, scrubbed one of Laurio's white shirts till her fingers bled and the shirt's cuffs whitened as if with the grace finding its way to Laurio's soul.

Nicky Coco

Nicolo Cococozzi, Nicky Coco. Mid-thirties, brown curls around a Saint Anthony bald spot, sleepy black eyes, and ears like Andy Panda. Twelve years back he married Emma, Don Patsy Stellato's older daughter.

The man and wife had both grown up in the neighborhood and in the camaraderie that made it what it was; the battles that chased away the brickbat warriors, mickey-finners, the Irish Tammany gangs; the *Mezzogiorno* guys who'd chased Arnold Rothstein's leg breakers, gamblers, loan sharks and heroin dealers to running their business someplace else.

The Italians had snatched the unions from Jews and Communists, put button-holers, hat makers, sewers and pressers into the same local with heavy equipment operators. Italians ran the streets, gambling and protection. Women sat in Columbus Park with their kids, walked to shopping, walked to midnight mass and walked home, and nobody went near them.

It was a tough neighborhood, but a made neighborhood, nobody moving out, nobody coming in without an okay. It was where Nicky never wanted to leave, since he was a kid, humping tubs of mortar for masons, staying clammed up about shakedowns, broken legs, strong armed labor, and other things he wished he didn't know.

He didn't smoke or gamble, kept his drinking to a glass of wine at dinner, and was a cinch to be a good father if Emma got pregnant again and, if she held it for three months, the doctor said, she would go the other six. She'd had two miscarriages and both times Nicky's nose bled till she came home from the hospital.

Emma leaned toward a kind of chubby that policed itself with the results of little sleep and a hurry-up way about her. Two years older than her sister, the pretty Antoinette, she was quicker with wit, sharper with figuring angles, and more emotional on the Baby Grand that still sat in the Stellato house where the sisters had learned to play it. Her face was small and soft, and, as Nicky learned twelve years past, the pretty in it took its time being noticed.

Nicky liked being on his jobs, breaking balls with his guys and bragging that he built his houses better than code. A layback, on-the-level guy whenever he could be, which was most of the time, and that's the way father-in-law Stellato urged him to be. But quick with a buck if the building inspectors needed a little something to help move the paperwork. "Everybody gotta eat, you know," he'd say with a throaty chuckle, and palm off a few fins.

In winter he wore a blue and black checkered lumber jacket and a cap with earmuffs that made him look dopey. But the man wasn't dopey, not the way he built, rented and sold rows of one, two and four family homes.

He and Emma lived in the downstairs in one of his houses, a two family with a garage in the back that used to be a carriage house. They had moved in during the last of reconstruction, weeks after the wedding and big deal reception. More than Nicky's idea of a reception, but Patsy picked up the tab and sent the honeymooners to the Caribbean. Emma's idea. They wanted babies and she figured palm trees, sun and ocean would keep Nicky working at it.

The house could have been a castle the way they treated it, coddled it like a breathing thing. Nothing ever stayed old or broken. The upstairs rooms, five of them, stayed vacant. They didn't need the rent money and Emma didn't like the idea of strangers living over their heads. And if she ever got all the kids she wanted ... *I mean, who knows*?

Anyway, Nicky, generous good guy, went along with his wife's funny ideas. But because of the empty upstairs, they picked up a cross. Sonny Burgundi.

On the evening after a day long and cold for guys out in the weather, the radio playing in the living room, the kitchen warm and steamy with Emma's lentil soup, she and Nicky sat to eat. Quietly, as usual, then Emma spoke.

"My father wants Antoinette upstairs after the wedding."

Nicky stared, as if he hadn't heard her.

"Nicky?" she said.

"And Sonny?"

"Of course, Nicky."

"Your father's worried about her?"

Emma shrugged in a way that said: *And what do you think?*

"What's the difference now? He already had reason to end this problem, but he let things go and now ... shit."

"You're right, Nicky. But my mother, she begged him, you know, as long as he doesn't hurt Antoinette ..."

"Yeah, yeah, and in the meantime, we carry the cross."

Nicky downed two glasses of wine that night.

So this peaceful house, this cherished home, where nothing stayed broken, got good and broken before Emma finished the dishes. And it stayed that way. Not with yelling, kicking and biting, but with the quiet that happens when a stranger stays too long.

But Emma did the right thing for the house. She invited her mother and her father, and Antoinette and Sonny for a Sunday dinner.

Antoinette got to Emma's kitchen early that day, coming downstairs in the green dress she had worn to mass, a little snug with new life growing. Her hair, like her mother's and her sister's, was almost black, or almost brown, but a color that allowed envious red highlights. Her face, not long, but longer and rosier than Emma's, had changed little since the face in her baby pictures.

Emma was standing at the stove, a splash of sauce at the front of her house dress.

"Where's Mama?" Antoinette asked.

"That dress looks nice on you. I didn't go to church today. You must have gone early."

"Yeah, where's Mama?"

"On the phone in the bedroom trying to find Daddy."

"We can't eat without him? He already said he's not coming, she should leave it alone."

Josephine came into the kitchen, took off her apron and tossed it to Antoinette. "Be careful with that dress. Don't get it dirty. You look so pretty."

"Thanks, Ma. What do you need me to do?"

"Set the dining room table, the table cloth is ... you know where it is. Bring in the meatballs and the gravy. Your father went for bread, the macaroni's going in. Where's Sonny?"

"He's coming down."

Nicky, the bread and a bottle of chianti got to the table as Sonny, a new smudge on his face that was supposed to be a moustache, came in, said hello to his mother-in-law and nodded to everybody else.

"Next week is spring," Antoinette said, letting go the breath she'd been holding while she watched her husband ignore everybody but her mother.

"Thank God," Josephine said. "So cold this year. No?"

"Emma, this gravy is good," Nicky said. "Your mother must have helped. Right Mama?"

"My son-in-law loves to tease his wife," Josephine said, talking to no one. She looked like Antoinette and laughed like Emma. "Not that I didn't help."

"Too bad your husband didn't come for dinner," Sonny said to her, his voice light, his eyes on the plate in front of him.

"He had something to do," Josephine said.

"I told you that, Sonny," Antoinette said, then nudged him.

"Oh, yeah, before I forget." He took an envelope from a hip pocket, slapped it on the table near Emma and said to Nicky: "Rent. Last month, this month, and next month."

"How nice," Nicky said.

Antoinette had once asked Sonny how he made money.

"Business."

"Business with Mootzi Tonno?"

"Yeah, sometimes he gets something."

"Like what, Sonny?"

"Just business, Antoinette. Just business."

When she and Emma were kids, still living in a two bed-room apartment, Mama yelled a lot and cried a lot. The argument Antoinette was remembering now came from the envelope on the table.

A Sunday back then too, the rooms quiet, dinner dishes put away, espresso pots and cups still on the kitchen table, Daddy polishing his shoes over the kitchen sink.

"You're going out?" Mama asked.

"Yeah, gotta go out."

"What's so important that you gotta go out on a Sunday night?" Mama asked, her hands in the dishwater.

"Again with this, Josephine? How many times? Things I don't talk about, Josephine. You should know that by now. Where's my shirt?"

"In the bedroom. Where you left it."

"You didn't press it?"

"I didn't know you needed it. You didn't tell me."

"What about a fresh collar?"

"In the drawer. When will you be back?" Josephine dried her hands as her husband walked away.

"When I get back," he called from the bedroom.

"Where you going?" She called after him, then, in the bedroom, "With that rotten son of a bitch Morello?"

"Look, what I gotta do, I do." He held an envelope for Josephine to see. "What you spend I don't complain." He dropped the envelope on the bed. "And watch your mouth."

Josephine got to watching her mouth pretty quick and she cried only when she was alone. The quiet got nice for Emma and Antoinette, always getting surprised with new furniture, clothes, the piano lessons.

* * *

Since her high school years, Antoinette had vowed to keep herself for her husband, that her first man would be her last. And there had been something comfortable about Sonny — he'd promised to marry her anyway — a familiarity that ran chills through her when he slapped the rent money on Emma's table.

How many times she told herself that she should have recognized him for what he was before she'd started sneaking out to meet him, before lying down with him and breaking a piece of her own vow, then desperately clinging to what remained of her first man being her last.

Besides, she'd reasoned even now, to not be married and have a baby would be shame for the family. Mama had agreed, but unlike Mama, Antoinette would never again ask her husband how he made his money.

Sonny had been coming home every night, and that was good, asking how she felt, any kicks today? You need something? But Antoinette had heard enough whispers between her father and his friends to make her wise. They all wanted something and Sonny wanted a button, wanted to be a soldier. And when she watched him figure that nobody would propose him, he faked a few months of interest to stay on the good side of things. Only his long face showed the world that it owed him a living.

Antoinette accepted her own doing and she plucked good from the bad. Like the pleasure in her belly and the security of this house — thank God for Nicky Coco — as near a home like the one where she and Emma — thank God for Emma too — had grown up.

Early in an afternoon she opened her door and called down the hall stairs.

"Emma? Ma, you here?"

"Yes," Josephine called back. She had been visiting almost every day since Antoinette and Sonny moved in. "You have the dress from Rose?"

"Yes, come up."

Antoinette stood at the top of the stairs, the dress on a hanger, the skylight making highlights in it.

Josephine, in a new dress of her own, looked up. "Oh, how nice, Antoinette."

"Rose did the whole thing herself," Antoinette said. "And she can take it in after the baby. See the pleats, how nice?"

Emma in pajamas and robe, curlers in her hair, stepped into the hall behind her mother. "That Rose is an artist." Then, climbing the steps quickly, said softly: "What the hell was that son of a bitch hollering about last night?"

"I don't know. Something went wrong and he takes it out on me. Did you tell Mama he was yelling?"

"No."

"Did Nicky say anything?"

"I don't think he heard. He didn't wake up."

"Ma, what are you waiting for? Come up," Antoinette said, and led them into the dining room, its tall windows looking down at the street, little girls on a stoop playing with dolls and carriages, boys in the gutter with bottle caps.

"Sit. I'll make coffee," Antoinette said.

"We just had," Josephine said, sitting at the table, shuffling in her chair to face Antoinette. "Let's talk about something."

Antoinette draped her dress over the easy chair at the windows, where she liked to sit listening to the radio.

"Okay, Ma, what are we talking about?" She sat at the table, a piece of smile on her face.

"Your father and I think it's a good idea for the colored girl to help out a little," Josephine said. "What's her name, Emma?"

"Bobbi."

Bobbi had helped Emma with housework during her pregnancies and miscarriages.

"I feel okay," Antoinette said. "Maybe when it gets closer."

"Seven months is close," Josephine said, a nervous laugh in her voice.

"I don't know, I mean ..."

"Your father'll pay for it."

"No, Sonny'll pay."

"Please, no problems."

"No. He'll pay if he knows what's good for him."

"There's something else," Josephine said. "I might as well say now, Antoinette."

"Yes?"

"The baby. Your father says don't name him after him."

"What?"

"Your father says don't name him after him."

Antoinette stiffened. "What the hell is that?"

"Yes, but wait. He says that Emma's the older one and her baby, and when the time comes — "

"If the time comes," said Emma.

"Her baby should be named after him first."

"So, both can't be named after him? That happens all the time, Ma. He doesn't know that?"

"That's what he wants in that thick head of his. That Emma is older, he means, you know," Josephine said.

"In other words my baby's a bastard of a mistake and my father, the gangster, makes no mistakes. New rules whenever he wants. He hates Sonny and he makes you tell me a story."

"Who's better to tell you? I mean, it's not a story."

Emma took Antoinette's hand and said: "Look, you said once that Sonny wanted to name the baby after Benny. Rose's Benny."

"Yes, he did," she said, "and I said: 'The baby gets named for my father. That's the way it works.' I told him, and he said okay. But forget it now. The hell with him."

"Don't talk like that, Antoinette," Josephine said. "You don't mean it."

Antoinette's eyes went from hard to sad to teary. "If it's a girl I can't name her after you either?"

Emma smiled. "It's a boy," she said.

"The gnome? Lina?" Antoinette said.

"Yes."

"Little Benny," Antoinette said, as if seeing him.

"That's not all," Josephine said, as if holding a secret. "You tell her, Emma."

"Tell me what?"

"What the gnome said, that if the neighborhood is saved, it will be by a boy of this house."

The Speak

Benny Bats walked into the site shack on Nicky's job.

Nicky looked up from the *Daily Mirror* sports page. "Hey, Benny, how you doing? Georgie told me you guys were coming around. Where is he?"

"He went to make a call."

"What do you think, there's no phones here?"

"We didn't know."

"He comes back, we go eat."

"No time," Benny said, eyeing Nicky's belly.

"I'm aggravated, I eat," Nicky said, his palms on his belt.

"Your brother-in-law?"

"My sister-in-law is an angel, God bless her, hooked up with a fucking misery. He don't even say hello, this lazy bastard. I gotta chase him for the fucking rent. I heard —"

"That door locked?" Benny asked, looking at the door he'd just come in.

"Yeah."

"What did you hear?"

"I heard him and Mootzi stepped on their dicks. They used Zito's name."

"You heard right. That's why I'm here."

"Yeah?"

"You gotta do something for us," Benny said.

"Don't tell me you want me to put them to work."

"No, no." Benny let go a chuckle, took a tear of paper from his pocket, gave it to Nicky. "Go look at this place. An apartment, a walk-in, it's empty, the door is open. See about making it a speak."

Nicky looked at the address. "Harlem."

"Yeah. Zito's good with it."

※ ※ ※

Carmine had told Benny: "These two clear heads, they got a spot up in Harlem for a club."

"Sonny told me," Benny said. "I told him to cop a mope."

"We're gonna do it."

Benny kept quiet long enough to be sure he'd heard right, and then be respectful. "Not for nothing, Carmine —"

"We're gonna do it. He's my fucking son." Carmine looked square into Benny's face. "What can I do?"

"Look, I go with whatever you say, no disrespect, you know that. But Zito. I mean, Harlem's his. These two did wrong by him and he did right by giving it to us to handle. But to give them a spot under his name?"

Carmine nodded. "I know, I know. But Zito knows the whole thing. We set it up, he calls it his, he gives them what they can't steal, he keeps the problems."

"He don't ask why?" Benny asked.

"I told you, he knows the whole thing. They give him headaches, he does what he does, and we got no say."

※ ※ ※

Nicky Coco drove into Harlem, up the side of a valley to Sugar Hill. He parked on Convent Avenue, walked into 143rd Street to a bottom apartment, alley entrance into a brownstone. He measured and sketched and found a phone in a candy store on the corner.

"Yeah, Benny, listen. I'm there now. The neighborhood ain't bad, the place could make a nice speak. But the rest of it's a whore house. A roulette wheel I seen, a crap table. You know that? All jigaboos. The guy who runs the place, colored guy too, came around. Nice guy. He owns the building, he says. Keeps it clean, quiet, gets along with the cops, he says."

"When you gonna start the job?"

"Whenever you say."

"Start."

* * *

Bar, tables, mirrors, colored lights. Sugar Hill went big for Sonny and Mootzi's spot that came to be known as *Mootzi's*. The two of them grew responsible, stayed on top of the bills, out of the tills, and on time with Mo Zito's cuts. They had a few dozen suits between them, nearly all from *LuciaRosina*. Sonny put on pounds, Mootzi seemed taller, and everything got good.

Things got good down in Nicky's house too. Sonny hardly came home. Not because of the whorehouse — he didn't like colored girls — but he laid down with the kind of dolled-up flappers fascinated with mob guys. And one in particular, a dream puss who looked like Clara Bow.

His face got to looking less sour, and he made good the rent to Nicky. He gave Antoinette whatever she needed, and she got to needing the colored girl, weeks before the baby got named and baptized Benito Burgundi by Uncle Nicky and Aunt Emma — and that happened about the same time the dream puss emptied a closet in her Riverside Drive apartment and hung suits and shirts in it for Sonny.

Bobbi

The colored girl, Bobbi Mercer. Talking, laughing and singing — always singing — from nine to whenever. She'd kept Antoinette rested and smiling right to the day Nicky drove her to the maternity ward. Bobbi stayed on, three days a week, and stayed late on Little Benny's first birthday. Hats, cake, candles, and *Happy Birthday to You.*

That night, Antoinette put the kid to bed, got into a robe and her chair at the window to watch a new snow, and dozed till a commotion at the front door sent her into the hallway. From the top of the stairs she looked down to see Emma whisking snow off an upright piano.

"Why's it smell of beer?" Emma asked Tulio Pastina, one of the three guys who'd hauled it in.

Tulio grinned, looked up to Antoinette. "Good kraut beer."

Emma said: "Come down, let's try it."

With Nicky and Emma and the three guys around her, Antoinette played chords.

"Needs tuning," Emma said.

"Not that bad," Antoinette said and kept playing. "Where should we put it?"

"We figure we put it up in the *stanzin',*" Nicky said. "Good up there, Antoinette?"

"Yes, good."

"Bring it up," Nicky told the guys.

Tulio, strong, even with legs pained with shrapnel, helped hump the piano up eleven steps to 'a *stanzin*', a small room in nobody's apartment at the top of the stairs.

They had the piano cleaned up, tuned up and refinished, and giggled when the low notes let go a smell of stale ale. The piano could have been family, the way they made it belong, Antoinette or Emma banging out songs the radio, the phonograph, or Bobbi taught them.

"Where'd you learn to sing like that?" Emma asked Bobbi.

"Just sing, that's all."

Months passed before Sonny got home enough to know Bobbi sang. Antoinette watched the way he ogled her like Barney Google, as if seeing her each time, for the first time, stacked and spirited, growling come-get-me notes that lit up her green eyes.

"She always sing like this?" Sonny asked, Antoinette seeing his eyes warm and excited as they'd once been for her.

"Always," Emma said.

"She comes here on time, does what she has to do?"

"Always."

"She's clean?"

"Yeah."

"Think she'd work the club?"

"Ask her."

* * *

Bobbi kept the Sugar Hill crowd drinking, dancing, and slapping fives and tens on the bar while Mootzi watched the biggest spenders hit on her.

The sun coming up one morning, Mootzi told her: "Sing is

what you do. Talk too. Tease is okay if it keeps them spending. But don't get involved, we don't need headaches."

"You telling me what to do now, but what gonna be when drinking get to be legal again?"

"When that happens we worry about it."

"But what you gonna do with me?"

He put a hand on her ass and a hand under her chin. "You keep singing and smiling, and keeping that sugar covered."

"'Cept for you, I suppose."

"You suppose right."

She wriggled close. "That a gun I'm feeling, or your bully bone is happy to see me?"

"Gun. Bully bone is later."

"What you need a gun for?"

"What do you think?"

"Don't be shooting nobody."

"Good idea."

"I be needing shoes."

He took a wad of bills from a pocket, peeled off a short stack. "Here. Get a dress too."

"What about when the dress don't fit no more?"

"What do you mean?"

She began a smile, then knocked it off. "You put a baby in my belly, Mootzi."

"Bullshit."

"Ain't bullshit."

"So," he said, shrugging, "get rid of it."

"Why I need to get rid of your baby if you love me like you says?"

"Get rid of it and shut the fuck up."

＊ ＊ ＊

Nicky getting home, Bobbi on the porch hanging laundry on the line, Emma coming out to the driveway.

"She says she's pregnant."

"So?"

"Mootzi's the father."

"So?"

"He don't want to know about it and she doesn't know what to do. She's afraid of him."

"Give her some money, chase her away."

"She doesn't want money."

"Abortion? Stay out of it."

"Mootzi sent her to a woman to do that. She didn't go; she wants a home for the kid."

"She got no family?"

"Aunts or something down south. Her mother's dead; she never knew her father."

"Let her go crying to Carmine."

"She says Mootzi would kill her. She just wants the baby in a good home."

Nicky's face went firm and he shook his head. "No, no, no, Emma. You can't do that. Your father puts up with enough shit around here and so do we. Now you want to bring a colored kid into this house? Don't even ask."

"Half colored."

"Look, she ain't our business. She helps out, we pay her, she goes home."

"She's been with us so long, Nicky."

"Emma, I'm telling you, forget it."

* * *

Months later, a morning cold and wet, Emma answered a knock on the door, found Bobbi standing there in a coat Antoinette had given her. Her lip bruised and busted, she held a bundle of baby in her arms.

"See my child, Emma," Bobbi said and moved a corner of a blanket from the baby's face. "Ain't she beautiful?

"Beautiful," Emma said. "So beautiful."

"Doctors say she gonna have green eyes like me. Beautiful child, and Mootzi don't wanna know about her," Bobbi said, talking quickly, her breaths short. "See my face, what he did. 'Ugly little nigger,' he calls her and he ain't never even seen her. Good baby, too. Don't cry but sometimes. I ain't got but some clothes and a diaper, but please let her be here."

"Bobbi, that can't be, I told you. Come inside," Emma said, then called up the stairs: "Antoinette, come down and see Bobbi's baby."

Bobbi stepped in. "Something bad awful gonna happen if she stay with me, Emma."

"What do you mean?" Antoinette asked, coming down the stairs. "What will happen?"

"Mootzi say he gonna kill me if I don't go away. But see my baby, Antoinette. She don't cry but sometimes." She handed the baby to Antoinette. "And the police say there ain't nothing they could do. He say he gonna kill me, but he gotta kill me before there be something to do about it."

"So stay here," Antoinette said.

"Just my baby to stay here. I got to go find my aunts. I ain't got nobody else."

"Where are they?"

"Don't know yet, but I'll come for my baby when I know."

"Mootzi's father won't let him hurt you."

"That man knowing is why he gonna kill me. He get crazy, he beat on me. Look at where he hit my mouth with his gun."

"Leave the baby with me."

"I don't know, Antoinette," Emma said. "Think about this —"

And Bobbi said: "Thank you, Antoinette. I find someplace to go and I call you." She kissed the baby and hurried away, the door closing on a final thank-you.

From Sugar Hill to the neighborhood, nobody doubted Mootzi for the baby's father. Nobody but Antoinette.

"Emma, you don't understand. Sonny maybe has something to do with this. You didn't see the way he was looking at her that night?"

"No, Antoinette. That's your imagination. She says Mootzi's the father. She should know. You better talk to Mommy."

"It doesn't matter what Mommy says."

"What about Sonny?"

"Up his ass."

"This is not his baby, Antoinette."

"Maybe no, maybe yes. And if it's a sister to my son, I can't turn my face."

"What about Daddy?"

"Just tell him I won't name her after him."

***

Bobbi couldn't come back. The super of her building on Lenox Avenue found a charred version of her in the coal furnace.

"Eye-Italian fella," he told detectives. "Got the speak up on the hill, Hunret-forty-three, Amsterdam. He pay her rent. Lovely girl don't make no trouble, ain't never hurt nobody."

"When was the last time you saw him?"

"Last night. First time in a long time. He be drunk and fussing and shit."

They looked for Mootzi, never found him.

Dominic Tonno Loves
Bernadina LaScala

Bernadina LaScala, the only child of a druggist and an art teacher, dressed better than most of the neighborhood women. She looked classy because she was classy. She stood taller than many of its men, and pretended little notice of their eyes following her wherever she went. She had grown up in the neighborhood, an apartment up on 10th Street — nice apartment, and a summer house up in the Bronx. A pale and baby-fat-chubby kid, until she turned seventeen and her hair took on a glisten on sunny afternoons, and her complexion brightened from olive to pink and white.

She had known Dominic Tonno since their mothers had taken them to masses at Christ the King Church, then to its school, where they spent eight years not noticing each other.

They went to different high schools, graduated on the same day, and the neighborhood saw them hand in hand, strolling beneath the lacelike arches of bulbs that brightened the gambling wheels and food stands at the street Feast of San Gennaro.

From the first days of this romance, to picking the maid of honor and the best man, family and friends reminded Bernadina that Dominic's father was Happy Carmine, that Patsy Stellato was his uncle, and that Dominic's future must take up a few pages in one of Lina's books.

Friends and relatives were probably right, so Bernadina avoided them. She would not break away from the handsome Dominic, his power and generosity, the respect others gave him and gave her because of him. Anyway, he said he loved her, bought a ring, and told her they would marry. If he had asked, she wouldn't have known what to say, so she put on the ring, picked a date, and started to make a baby.

* * *

Ever since he could remember, Dominic Tonno wanted to be like his father. Both stood the same five and a half feet tall (an inch or so shorter than Bernadina) walked with the same strut, and carried the same gaze in eyes as blue as the sapphires they both wore on their fingers. His head was less square than his father's, and his teeth more white; his mother had told him not to smoke, and maybe that was why he didn't. His hair whitened soon after marrying, and stayed an attraction to the impressive and obedient Bernadina who gave Dominic a boy.

Dominic never denied respect for his father, though at times the father needed to remind him that respect involved patience, and that doing the right thing wasn't always the right thing. Like after brother Mootzi disappeared.

"Mootzi's not around, we don't know what happened," Dominic had said, "and we don't say boo. It ain't right, Pop."

"Zito didn't do anything we didn't expect," Carmine said.

"Yeah, but what about Sonny? What did he do that's so right?"

"He didn't kill anybody, that's what he did. Your Uncle Patsy don't like him, didn't want him near Antoinette, but he went soft because that's what he does for his kids."

"And that's right?"

"I didn't say it was right."

"Yeah, well, from what I hear, Antoinette don't care what happens to her husband."

"It ain't our business, Dominic, and there's other things I got on my mind right now."

Other things like the cancer in his mouth from those greasy black stogies that he still puffed down to stubs. And on his mind was Dominic and the future.

"Mootzi never gave a fuck about Dominic," he had told Patsy Stellato, "but Dominic always did the right thing for him. Protected him, got him out of shit that I didn't want to get him out of, and Dominic never talked about it."

"Dominic's a good boy."

"Who knows how long I got, and so I ask you how he stands."

"Yeah, well, your wife came to my house," Stellato said.

"Yeah?"

"She's your wife, she's my wife's sister, I listen to her. She says I'm the uncle, she already lost one son, and with all the aggravation that he was, she would die to lose the other, and I should chase him from this life."

"I hear the same thing," Carmine said.

"I told her you're the father, you got a lot on your mind, but I said I'll talk with you. The thing is, Carmine, I got nothing to say about what you do with this, but you tell me what I could do. Hide him or help him make his way up."

"You know what I want."

* * *

In the meantime, what was going on with Sonny, nobody cared, not even Aunt Rose. Since before Prohibition he avoided her and his mother, slow, gray and bent. Whatever they could do for him wasn't worth scheming for. Lucia talked and smiled whenever she recognized him, and a mumble came out of her mouth that annoyed him into a scowl.

Aunt Rose had turned on him, saying that he did nothing for his mother while for years she fed and washed her, ran the business, and worried about him for her.

He knew from years back that Benny Bats had no use for him, so forget about a score coming out of there. He stopped wishing his mother dead, there was no percentage in it.

After Prohibition ended, he talked to Mo Zito about making the speak an after hours joint. Zito turned him down, but okayed a loan through one of his crew — one point a week back then — and picked up one of the old spots in the neighborhood. It went good for a few years, paid the rent for him and the used-to-be flapper, too old now to look like Clara Bow, but young enough to write checks that covered the vig, and then the principal on the loan.

But the connection to Patsy Stellato, father-in-law or not, broke in a lot of places, and no matter how broke it got, it still kept him safe from stickups and shakedowns, made him feel protected, got him walking like a rooster to Nicky's house once or twice a week, slap an envelope on Antoinette's kitchen table, try to get laid, and slam the door on his way out when he didn't.

One night, Stellato up in Saratoga with his wife and the racetrack, Antoinette turned down Sonny and this time he didn't slam the door.

She wouldn't scream, wouldn't scare Little Benny or baby Bobbi, both asleep in their rooms, but she got slapped and tossed around like she was a dishrag. She went for the phone, he ripped it from the wall. She went for the door, he spun her, slapped and punched her face as if she were a man, and ran down the stairs.

Nicky out in the hall. "Hey. What the hell's going on up there? Why you gotta slam that fucking door like that? What's the matter with you?"

"Ah, I get pissed off, you know."

"Give me the key to the house."

"I live here, my kid, my wife."

"You don't live here. Give me the key. When your father-in-law tells me to give it back, you'll get it."

Sonny gave up the key and beat it out the front door.

Nicky called up the stairs: "Antoinette, you all right?"

She opened her door and stepped back, out of the light. "Yeah, Nicky, I'm okay. Thanks."

"We gotta get rid of that son of a bitch. The kids are okay?"

"Yeah, thanks."

Nicky didn't know Antoinette had caught a beating until next morning. Black eyes, bruises, puffed lips. No phone call to her father, but something better. The kind of better that made a neighborhood legend they still talk about.

Nazis End the
Problem of Sonny

Nicky Coco's face goes wide and bright when he tells the story:

Yeah, so, Tulio Pastina, the guy with the bad legs — German shrapnel, 32nd Division, Alsace — one of the guys who brought us the piano from the speakeasy uptown, worked for me before and after the war, during and after Prohibition, whenever I needed him. The guy is a master with finished work. Cabinets, moldings, staircases, like that, like magic.

His legs aren't his only problem. He's got this wife that needs doctors — special doctors — all the time, and he goes for his lungs with bills. When he has no work with carpentry, or even when he does, he drives a cab for extra cash. Gotta have a lot of respect for the guy, working the way he does, with legs in the pains all the time, reminding him to hate krauts.

One day he calls me, and a half hour later he wheels a cab into one of my Bronx jobs. I'm in the shanty looking out the window. He gets out of the cab, he's wearing the cabdriver cap, old army boots, and a peacoat. He looks old, but he's younger than me. His face says he's hurting, but he's stepping pretty quick.

"Come in, Tuli, I got us sandwiches," I tell him.

"I ate at my mother's just now. But I'll take it to my wife later."

"How's your legs?"

"Same."

"What's up that you can't talk on the phone?" I ask him.

"First Avenue, Eighty-ninth," he says.

"Germantown," I say.

"This kraut gets in the cab, I take him up the Bronx, White Plains Road. He gives me a fin and an envelope. He don't know me, but I know him. The piano we brought to your house?"

"Yeah?"

"It came from a joint on Eighty-fifth, a kraut joint that got torched before we got you that piano. I took fares there a few times. Cheap fucks. That's how I seen this guy, either I took him there in the cab, or maybe I seen him on the street up there."

"And?"

"He tells me bring something up to Decatur Avenue. Okay, I take the fin and the envelope." Tulio turns, shuts the shanty door. "Fifty grand."

"In the envelope?"

"I wish. Then I wouldn't be here."

"Then what?"

"Before I go to Decatur with the envelope, I go to my mother's house, steam open the envelope, maybe there's some spy shit in there."

I'm laughing at him. "Spy shit."

"Why, it can't be?"

"Keep going."

"It's in English, a shakedown. Fifty fucking grand getting delivered."

Tulio waits, watching me like making sure I'm paying attention. He always does that.

"Yeah, and?"

"So I go to Decatur. I don't know if this guy's the pigeon or *what, but I give him the envelope. 'What's your name?' he wants to know. I tell him Angelo. He says, 'Italian.' I says 'yeah,' and he says, 'come in.'"*

"I go in, he opens the envelope, reads the letter, and gives me another five spot. Old guy, seventy, seventy-five. A little pat-so. Says he needs somebody with him when he gives something to some guy, that it's worth a deuce."

"Anybody else know this?"

"Who's gonna know?"

"Who is this guy?"

"I don't know. He's acting like in the movies, you know, spy shit. He gives me his phone number, I should ask for Jafsie and he'll know who I am."

"Daffy."

"No. Jafsie, but daffy too."

"That's it?"

"That's it. What you think?"

"When you gotta get back to him?"

"I figure right away, no?"

Even though I'm not in a crew, my father-in-law is Pat Stel-lato, boss of the neighborhood crews. So, I gotta stay on the level, be careful for him. To do things right, I need his okay, maybe not for the two hundred, but for whatever was going on with the fifty grand. And with him up in Saratoga, and because things can't wait, I figured I'm near enough to being legit, plus he knows I keep my mouth shut.

"Want me to call now?" Tulio asks.

I slide the phone to him and get half the conversation.

"Yeah, Jafsie? Me, the cab driver."

Tulio writes on a pad on the desk. "Tomorrow, yeah. Call you. What? Angelo. I told you. They call me Angelo." Tulio looks at me, makes a funny face.

"Okay, I'll call tomorrow," Tulio says, hangs up, and he's nodding and grinning like a kid. "He wants for us to hook up with him and this other guy."

"Who's the other guy?"

"Who knows?"

"I don't know, Tuli ..."

"If we don't do this, we'll never know what we threw away."

"Yeah."

"You got something?" Tulio asks.

"Yeah, but I don't wanna shoot nobody. You got something?"

Tulio smiles. "Remember that Luger I showed you?"

"I remember."

"See you tomorrow," Tulio says.

"And don't forget the sandwich for your wife."

* * *

I meet up with Tulio, he's got the cab, we drive to one of the quiet streets around Westchester Square in the Bronx, nobody around. We wait till a beat up Ford with a rumble seat shows up, passes by a few times, then parks.

A tall guy, white shirt, tie, dark fedora and overcoat, comes out of nowhere.

"That's him," Tulio says.

"Jafsie?"

"Yeah."

Jafsie gives Tulio a nod and gets in the Ford. We get a quick gander at the guy driving, he pulls out, we follow. Over to the westside, down Riverside Drive in Manhattan, they stop. Jafsie makes a call on a street phone, gets back in the car. They stop and call, two, three more times.

"They're being careful," Tulio tells me, as if I don't know. "Looking for a set up or something."

I say: "This looks like bullshit."

"No, Nicky. No."

We stay with the Ford back up to the Bronx, Tremont Avenue. The cemetery, Saint Raymond's. The Ford parks, shuts the lights, near a guy on a bench in a shadow. Jafsie gets out of the Ford, talks with the guy, goes back to the car, opens the rumble seat, takes a toolbox. He brings it to the guy on the bench and that guy gets in a gray Plymouth with the box, some other guy driving. I don't know where the Ford goes.

The Plymouth pulls out and now it don't look like bullshit. Jafsie starts walking to Tulio and I tell him: "Forget the two hundred, Tulio. Don't lose that box."

Tulio's calm, a real pleasant look on his face that fills the car with a caper so thick that you could taste it. I'm getting scared, I never did this kind of thing, but it would take more balls to call it off than to snatch fifty grand from scumbag krauts.

We stay with the Plymouth and they're moving slow, then fast, then slow. Tulio hangs loose. The Plymouth moves up White Plains Road, turns into 222nd Street. Tulio turns, pulls over, waits for the Plymouth to get through the block, but it pulls into a driveway.

"Now, Tuli," I say and he's already flooring it up the street, into the driveway, the krauts getting out. We get out. Tuli goes into a crouch, his luger gleaming and pointed like Action Comics. I'm so scared, I'm like a dimwit, but the guys in the Plymouth freeze.

"Put the box on the ground," Tulio says. He's sharp and quick, and I'm getting that way too.

The guy puts the box down.

"Put your hands on your head and back off," Tulio says.

The guys back off.

"How much is in there?"

"I don't know." The guy's got the accent, and I'm hoping Tulio don't shoot, he's a wacky guy right now, with this hate look in his

eyes, his finger on that fucking trigger — that if these krauts could know what this guy's been through, and what's on his mind — forget about it.

Anyway, he stays ready for anything, the way he musta been in a foxhole or something. And he says: "I think there's ten thousand in there."

"Yes, ten thousand," the kraut says.

"That's good. The ten is yours, the rest is ours. We don't talk about you and you don't talk about us. Or we take the whole fucking thing."

"We take ten."

❊ ❊ ❊

I stash the money. And it's a good thing, because my father-in-law wants to know if the forty grand that's left is in gold certificates.

"Some, yeah," I say.

"Where is it?"

"In the toolbox, in the garage."

"All of it?"

"Yeah, we waited for you before we did anything."

"The money's hot, the toolbox probably is too."

"Yeah?"

"Ransom money."

"Lindbergh?" I ask.

"Yeah. Find Sonny, call me when you got him."

❊ ❊ ❊

Jersey cops found the baby in the woods near the Lindbergh house, figured his head was bashed in right after the snatch. Bronx cops found the toolbox in the trunk of Sonny's car out by the Orchard Beach camp tents. Found Sonny in the trunk too, stinking up the camp, one behind the ear.

Police Commissioner Mulrooney tied a ribbon around the story. He told the papers that the toolbox had held the ransom money, had been marked for ID by Lindbergh and a Doctor John Condon — called himself Jafsie — and the murder was a message that the mob executed one of its own for being in on "the kind of atrocity unacceptable, even to the Italians."

* * *

Sonny's spirit whisked through Nicky's house in a few minutes of gasps and moans, tears of shock and few of sorrow. Then three days in one of the Patarama parlors, only Rose looked beat up, and that was because Grandma Lucia broke out of a stare and into a grief howl each time she recognized her son in the coffin.

Antoinette kept from smiling, but that's about all. Suspicions that her father had something to do with the kill must have breezed through her mind, making her feel like she had ordered the hit and wondered, along with Emma and Josephine, what happened to the box with the money.

Indictments

When detectives snatched Nicky Coco on his way to a job, he figured the krauts made a beef. But the story that spread through the neighborhood and across three or four newspaper pages had nothing to do with krauts.

Pictures in later editions showed guys from crews all over the city cuffed and herded through brass and glass doors of 100 Centre Street. From a holding cell in the basement, detectives brought them up to the District Attorney's Office, then fed them, one at a time, into a long room bright with tall windows, and two dozen Grand Jurors who watched them dumb up at questions about "Montovano Zito, head of the Zito Family"; "Pasquale Stellato, head of the Morello Family"; "Carmine Tonno, his Consiglieri,"; and "Dominic Tonno, in line to replace the aging Pasquale Stellato."

They put Nicky Coco on first, threw questions at him about guys and things he didn't know, and about the *Mezzogiorno Social Club* and bookmaking, loansharking, boxing and race-track fixes, bid rigs for city construction jobs. Things Nicky knew some answers to and said he didn't.

About union dues, pension money and faked books, he knew nothing. He knew nothing about hits and strong arms, guns and missing persons. Still he trembled under his old and frayed blue and black checkered jacket, thinking the DA must have figured he did. But he looked square at the grand jury and answered questions, his face open and sinless.

"Do you know Cesare Strachi?"

"Knew him. Everybody knew him."

"And he was killed?"

"That's what the papers said. Years ago."

"Do you know who killed him, or who saw to it that he was killed?"

"I couldn't know that."

"You know that his body was found in a milk truck abandoned in front of Police Headquarters?"

"I was a kid."

"Answer the question please."

"I don't know."

"Do you know Tomasso Petto?"

"No."

"Known as The Ox?"

"Yeah, yeah, I heard the name."

"Do you know where he is?"

"I heard you guys got him this morning."

"So you do know him."

"Yes."

"How do you know him?"

"Just seen him around."

"What does he do?"

"He used to be with Strachi, drove Strachi, but I don't know what he's doing now."

"Do you know Giorgio Pugliese?"

"Georgie Nuts?"

"You know him?"

"I know who he is."

"What does he do?"

"Peanuts. I mean he sells them."

"Was it he or Petto who left Strachi's body at Police Head-quarters?"

"How could I know that?"

"Answer the question please."

"I don't know."

"Did Dominic Tonno kill Cesare Strachi?"

"I don't know."

"Did Carmine Tonno kill Cesare Strachi?"

"I don't know."

"Does Mr. Pugliese do anything besides sell peanuts?"

"Not that I know."

"Have you ever placed a bet with Mr. Pugliese or anyone in the gambling operation that he controls?"

"I don't gamble."

"You never played the lottery? Policy? Numbers?"

"Once. I didn't hit and I never played again."

"With George Pugliese?"

"No, some guy at a job. A mason, I think he was."

"Who else have you placed bets with?"

"Nobody."

"Have you known Mr. Pugliese to oversee the gambling interests of Pasquale Stellato, Benito Carlucco, Carmine Tonno and Dominic Tonno?"

"Carmine's dead now. I don't know those other guys."

"You don't know Patsy Stellato?"

"My father-in-law, yeah. Sorry, I'm nervous."

"Are you a member of a union?"

"I'm a contractor. They say I don't have to be."

"Who runs the union to which you don't belong? Strike that. To what union would you be a member?"

"You mean the local?"

"Very well, the local."

"I don't know."

"Are your employees union members?"

"That's not my business. They're all their own contractors."

"Do you know Mr. Vito San Martino, Vito Red?"

"Real old guy. He's a boss or something with the unions. He negotiates pay. But I don't know him."

"Do you know Mr. Benito Carlucco?"

"No."

"Benny Bats?"

"No."

"Has Mr. Carlucco ever secured building contracts for you?"

"I make my own contracts."

"Has Mr. Carlucco, Mr. Pugliese, or Mr. San Martino visited your construction sites?"

"No."

"Thomas Petto?"

"No."

"Are you sure?"

"A lot of people visit."

"Do you know that lying to a grand jury could cost you a year or more in prison?"

"I don't know any of that."

"Do you wish to change any of your answers?"

"No."

"Request that the witness be remanded."

❈ ❈ ❈

Weeks on Riker's Island, Nicky Coco lay in a cell he shared with a guy from Brooklyn, and photos taped on the wall not as vivid as the photos taped on his memory.

There was the one of Little Benny, eight years old, skinny and wiry and sharp, running around Emma's kitchen the night Nicky came in with boxes of Chinese food and bottles of somebody's home made wine for the celebration. Emma was pregnant, and had been for three months.

"We still got six months to go and this place sounds like a nursery already," Nicky joked, happy all over his face.

Then the picture of Emma hugging Little Benny, Antoinette holding Bobbi's little girl in her arms, wailing for whatever she was needing. Then pictures from weddings, Christmases, the beach.

Nicky had about ten months left to do for the Contempt of Court and wasn't the only guy doing it. Georgie Nuts was with him. They all had the same lawyer, they all stayed clammed. Patsy Stellato had okayed plenty of grease for the system to smooth the way to take-it-easy. He copped Nicky and Georgie to year long misdemeanors and entered a not-guilty for Vito, Dominic and Benny. They made bail, got adjournment dates for a motion, and would, the lawyer said, cop them out in front of a right judge after the beef got too stale for the newspapers.

The investigation had begun in the office of Mayor Fiorello LaGuardia, politician and lawyer for workers and immigrants since before the stocks crashed and the depression got to be called great. He'd gotten himself made mayor with promises of jobs, welfare, housing and blue skies. He was an Italian Jew who spoke English, Italian and Yiddish. He promised to tear down blocks of spit and cardboard tenements and replace them with fourteen floors of bricks and subsidized rents.

The American newspapers called him *the Little Flower*.

He said Hitler was a maniac, Mussolini saddened him, and construction made jobs. Said it over and over in *Mondo Nuovo,* one of the newspapers friendly to him. Stellato's unions and contractors were good with the hokeydoke, and *Fiorello LaGuardia for Mayor* signs popped up all over the city.

But a new DA, a guy named Dewey, had been chasing after guys like Stellato and Zito, and was building a high profile with weak cases in splashes of politics for himself and the celebrity mayor. LaGuardia's projects would be built on the level. Clean unions, open books. No price fixes, no bid rigs, no kickbacks.

In Nicky's second month in Riker's Island, Emma, pale and her eyes sunk in shadow, visited. Six feet from each other, they looked through glass and talked by phone. She had more gray than he'd remembered.

"How'd you get out here?" Nicky asked, his eyes ringed with jailhouse dim. His hair had thinned since sitting in front of the Grand Jury, he needed a shave and his shirt hung loose from his shoulders.

"Benny drove," Emma said.

"Little Benny?"

"Big Benny. He wants to see you."

"You came just with him?"

"Rose too."

"They getting married?"

"She says no, but then she says not yet."

"What's he want with me?"

"I don't know."

"Look, Emma, I don't want you out here with all these animals. Less than a year I'll be out."

"A year is so long."

"Before you know it, it's over. Everything okay with my son?"

Emma's face brightened. "*Your* son? What about me?"

"*Our* son, yeah." Nicky smiled, his eyes damp.

"Little Patsy's a good boy, Nicky. Everybody says he looks like you. Four years old and with the radio all the time."

"His ears look like me too?"

Emma smiled, stifled a chuckle.

"What's the doctor say?" Nicky asked.

"He says he finds nothing wrong with him, that maybe he's just slow to learn."

"The way he remembers all the words to the songs? All the radio shows? You told him that?"

"He doesn't know what that means and he says don't worry. So don't worry. I meant to bring pictures, I forgot."

"Mail them."

"You lost so much weight, Nicky."

"The food's garbage. I don't even eat sometimes."

"I worry so much."

"Nah, they treat me good, got me and Georgie with all Italians. The kids know where I am?"

"They see the paper, hear the talk. Little Benny wants to know if he can use your car. He's going for his license."

"He's doing good with the horn?"

"He practices all the time."

"What about a job?"

"My father says he'll put him through school, be a lawyer."

"Forget about what your father says. See where I am because your father says? The kid needs to make it on his own, keep away from people like your father ... Sorry, Emma, I didn't mean that."

Emma looked away. "It's okay." She looked back. "Antoinette says his music teacher says he's doing good."

"The little girl asks about me?"

"Antoinette says she'll come next time with her and Little Benny."

"No, no. Don't make nobody come here. I'll be home before you know it."

"If that's what you want. You need anything?"

"Just pictures."

"I miss you, Nicky."

"Me too. Tell everybody I'm doing good."

Nicky turned to the guard. "Okay, Timmy."

"You got another."

"Oh, yeah, okay."

It surprised Nicky that it felt good to see Benny Bats, hear his voice.

"Nicky."

"Yeah, Benny. Thanks for bringing my wife. But please, don't let nobody bring her here. Okay?"

"I thought you would like it."

"Yeah, but no. No more. Okay?"

"Okay. How you doing?"

"How am I doing?" Nicky slapped his chest. "Here's how I'm doing. Look what you're wearing, look what I'm wearing. Ever seen me skinny like this?"

"It ain't over for me yet, either," Benny said. "You'll be out before I go in. I go back to court, they keep moving dates around. Me, Vito, Dominic, because things are happening and there's all new rules and we gotta fix things. The mayor's pushing for more projects and nobody wants to lose what's coming."

"I read the papers."

"We're in, you're in."

"I'm in? Then what am I doing here?"

"This had to happen. Things went good. Nobody squawked —"

"Yeah? Where's The Ox?"

"The Feds got him."

"They could name these projects after him. Where they got him?"

"Some army post. They wanna know about us, but things are still the same for us. Different corporations, you know, like that. But big things from now on, no wood frames."

"Nobody broke my balls with wood frames."

"What we got now could last us for life."

"I never got in trouble with wood frames. How come I'm in on this?"

"Patsy always pushed for you, only thing now, we got most of it. The mayor wants it. Supposed to be his last."

"Little commie prick fucking up the neighborhood like he fucked up Harlem and Brooklyn."

"We build, or somebody else does."

"Right in the middle of the neighborhood, fucking shame."

"Nobody wants projects," Benny said, "but they'll take the work."

"And fuck the neighborhood."

"We're in for foundations, concrete, doors and windows. You know what that means. Zito got the steel, but if we get in this fucking war, forget about steel."

"What about my houses? My simple fucking houses."

"We got the okay for twenty-two."

"The Bronx? The lots from the old racetrack you said we couldn't get?"

"Couldn't happen if we weren't out there. Hey, I seen Patsy. A big kid already. A nice kid."

"Looks like me, my wife says."

"Just like you."

"Hey, Benny?"

"Yeah?"

"Look, I don't want no part of this projects shit. Keep me out."

"Nicky, don't say that to Patsy."

❉ ❉ ❉

Nicky hadn't meant it when he told Emma that the year would go fast. But it did, maybe being locked in Riker's Island kept him from seeing LaGuardia's buildings. Typical government, thick, no class, no character, a brick by brick scheme of politicians and mob guys collecting votes and cash and making shadows on the neighborhood.

Late in the night they met in a restaurant. Nicky, Benny, and Patsy Stellato. Stellato's moustache white and still flowing, getting old but staying sharp, he said: "Nicky, you look good. It's good to see you."

At meetings like this, Stellato was not Nicky's father-in-law. He was boss.

"Good to see you guys," Nicky said.

"Just in time you got here," Stellato said. "You're our eyes and ears with this thing. None of us wanted anybody else. A lot of envy from everybody, we need you there."

"Sure, Patsy, sure."

"Meet up with Vito, lots of new things happening with the unions that you need to know."

Every day Nicky lumbered to the construction site as if toting a hod of mortar on each shoulder. He handled some of the labor problems himself, but unions were always looking for a shake, and he had to get that fucking Vito involved. And if the city inspectors broke balls, he called Benny.

But when the projects got to hovering high enough to see

from his windows at home, he had nobody to call. He pulled down shades. He found little difference between the projects and the misery he'd been in for a year. Not only in the shadows they threw, but both places had ways of keeping his spirit locked up. And there'd be no comfort from the same guys who made the neighborhood and now were stuffing their pockets by betraying it.

War, Swing, Doowop

Pearl Harbor. Neighborhood flags waving from walls and roof tops, stoops and porches. Kids getting drafted or joining up.

Brown-suited Western Union boys pedaled bikes. Where one of them stopped and plucked an envelope from the basket on the handlebars, people knotted around. A father had been wounded, a brother missing, a son killed; a gold star in the window for their lives.

No gold stars yet hung in the windows of Nicky Coco's house, but the bulk of talk shifted from the projects to Little Benny, old enough to get the greetings letter. Bring underwear, socks, toothbrush.

Before light on a damp summer morning, all the women crying in the house, he walked with Uncle Nicky and little cousin Patsy to Whitehall Street and the building with stained bricks and cloudy windows. On the stoop men and boys stood smoking, drinking coffee, waiting, as if the war would be over that morning and they'd all get sent home.

"Okay," Benny said. "Guess I better go in."

"Okay," Little Patsy said.

"Maybe it won't be long, Benny," Nicky Coco had said before, said it again, and handed Benny a few twenties. "You need something, call, write, whatever. Okay, Benny?"

"Okay, Uncle, thanks."

"Stay out of trouble."

Benny kissed them.

"You're gonna write us letters, right?" Little Patsy asked.

"Soon's I got something to write about."

* * *

By the time Benny got his first stripe, Little Patsy started first grade, Sacred Heart School. All Italian kids, no trouble pronouncing Cocococozzi. But they called him Cogootz. Like the squash. Quiet, sluggish and harmless, tallest in the class, slowest to learn. But with the prayers of his mother and Aunt Antoinette, and the prayers and patience of the nuns, he struggled through the first and second grades.

His second year in third grade, he started stealing what he didn't need. Crayons and pencils from other kids, chalk from the blackboard, ice and coal off trucks; comic books from the candy store and, lately, bottles of coffee soda that Emma wouldn't buy for him because the sugar and caffeine got him to being Superman, up and down the hall steps crashing down the bottom three, then four, then five. Superman on the fly protecting cousin Benny from Jap and Nazi fighter planes.

Dondadondon. Faster than a speeding bullet. Dondadondon. More powerful than a locomotive. And Emma calling from the kitchen: "Oopha, Patsy, stop. You're breaking the house. Don't come crying to me when you get hurt. Don't you have homework?"

Even without coffee soda Patsy talked or sang and entertained, kept the house laughing and cheering for more.

"Patsy, do Jimmy Durante."

"Do Al Jolson."

"He's got some imagination, this kid. Do Ethel Merman."

He'd speak with the voices of the radio back then, talking and giggling with the friends of his imagination. Gene Autry, Roy Rogers, the Green Hornet, Flash Gordon. Emma heard them, and at first went looking for them, as if to find Gene or Roy or Flash, and found only Patsy, on the steps in the hall, up in the music room, or in front of hers and Nicky's bedroom mirror.

He watched for the mail every day. On the days a letter came from Benny, he brightened, then dimmed till the next letter with a message like:

> Tell Patsy that there's no war in Alabama yet, but we all have rifles. They gave me a sax too. I don't know what it means, but they gave me the charts to the songs from the Glenn Miller books. He's here, you know. Will I get to play with him? Imagine.

Lunch time in Antoinette's kitchen, a bowl of marinara sauce, meatball sandwiches and glasses of milk, Bobbi's daughter, Bobbi, said: "Patsy never talks, Ma."

"Yeah, he's quiet. Did you tell him to come up and eat?"

"Yeah, but he was talking to Dick Tracy in front of Aunt Emma's bedroom mirror."

"At least he talks to somebody."

"I think he does his talking with the songs he sings."

"That's interesting for you to say," Antoinette said.

"He says he feels safe when he sings or when the radio's on."

"It's good to feel safe. Don't you think?"

Bobbi spooned sauce on her sandwich. "Sure."

"He's a special kind of kid. So are you."

"I'm not a kid. I'm 17."

"Right, I mean special from when you were a kid."

"Benny likes songs too, but he always talked with me."

"Yes, I know."

"Too bad he's not my real brother. I really miss him."

"I do too."

"Ma?"

"Yes?"

"I think about my real mother."

"It's okay if you do."

"Uncle Nicky always says I look like her. Do I?"

"Uncle Nicky says? Everybody says. Every day you look more and more like her. Green eyes and all."

"Sometimes I think she's in the music room."

"She must be happy to hear you play the piano."

"Patsy says she's more happy when I sing."

Antoinette smiled. "That's nice to think, but how could he know that?"

"Sometimes he talks with her."

"He's got some imagination."

"That's good, right?"

"That's good, right."

* * *

Spring, 1946. Duffle bag on his shoulder, Sergeant Benny Burgundi got off the subway at Brooklyn Bridge, climbed to the street, looked around and found the projects he'd read about in letters.

Into a playground, kids mobbed him, grabbed at him.

"You kill any Nazis?"

"You're a sergeant, right?"

"Kill any Japs?"

Benny had never seen a Jap or a Nazi. From Whitehall Street he'd been loaded on a bus with a few dozen recruits, express to Fort Dix, New Jersey. A few days of skull tests, a few months of basic training, an M-1 rifle and a sharpshooter badge. And, finally, Montgomery, Alabama, a tarnished horn and a seat in the sax section of Major Glenn Miller's Army Air Force Band and a run overseas.

"Easy with that, New York. Stick to what's written." Miller could be a pain in the ass.

"Yes sir, but only some of the music is on the sheet."

"Yeah, I know all about it. But in this band it's all on the sheet."

"Yes sir."

Benny walked on, turning again to see the projects, and searching for what hadn't changed. Familiar faces looked older. Radios in windows played songs he'd never heard. And Bobbi, not knowing he was coming home, left some guy talking to himself and raced to Benny, crying and laughing and hanging on as if to keep him from going back.

They walked, her arm in his. She no longer felt like a sister to him. He studied what her mother must have looked like. The chin, the nose, the smile, the green eyes — especially the eyes — then later, singing those songs new to him, and talking English with spatters and gestures of *napulitan'*.

In a neighborhood where people complained about the projects bringing in the coloreds, and scowling at Italians who married Irish, they stayed quiet when Benny left with Bobbi in Nicky Coco's Hudson, and days later came back with wedding rings.

❈ ❈ ❈

On a Sunday morning, cold and windy, Little Benny looked in the window of the *Mezzogiorno Social Club* past the fading colors of San Gennaro. Guys sitting around, playing cards, reading the paper, much of what he remembered. He went in, saw pictures on the wall, some new: Frank Sinatra, Perry Como, Louie Prima at a mike stand with his trumpet and an arm around a woman in a dress that looked like silver.

"That's up on Fifty-second Street. Your Uncle Nicky bought your Aunt Rose all his records."

Benny turned. "Uncle Benny." They hugged, shook hands.

"How you doing, kid?"

"Good, good."

"Made it home."

"Yeah."

"Aunt Rose told you to come see me?"

"Yeah, I asked about you."

"She looks good, huh?"

"She looks good. She misses my Grandma, I think."

"Yeah, but now she's got her own life."

"How'd Grandma die? Nobody talks about it."

"Nobody knows. They didn't want an autopsy. Your Aunt Rose says that for years after your Uncle Sonny died —"

"Died, huh?"

"Like you said, some things nobody talks about."

"Yeah, sorry, Uncle."

"After he died, grandma kept asking for him. Then she stopped asking and stopped eating. Let's go in the back." Benny Bats led Little Benny into the kitchen, Sunday sauce on the stove.

"That lady, Philomena, still cleans up?" Little Benny asked.

"Yeah, she can't stop working. Still works in the church too," Benny Bats said. "What was I saying? Oh yeah. In the

hospital they found nothing wrong, then one day, we went to
see her, she didn't know we were there. We left, she died."

"Yeah, that's what I heard. You and Aunt Rose getting married?"

"She wears a ring I bought years ago and that's enough.
But you and Bobbi ... congratulations. Living with your mother for a while."

"Yeah, for now. Still gotta get married in the Church."

"Got something for you," Benny Bats said, and handed
Little Benny a business card. "Go see them. They know who
you are."

❋ ❋ ❋

Decca Records, a studio band, sixteen, twenty pieces, depending
on who showed up. Benny on tenor and baritone. He did a few
gigs with some of the guys, bass, guitar, drums, pulled Bobbi
in on piano, got to calling her Bobbi Mercer — *sounds showbiz*,
said an agent. *And vocals, if you want to sell records.*

After doing back up sessions for Ruth Brown and Laverne
Baker, the *Ben Burgundi Band featuring Bobbi Mercer* released
a few sides of blues, jump and swing, got the jockeys to spin
them, Benny sensing a kind of persuasion he didn't need to
know about.

Billboard called it *Rhythm and Blues*, and *Rock 'n' Roll*.
They did one night stands, north, then south, where one guy
said: "We didn't know she was colored."

"You been hearing our records, you been hearing her sing.
Sure is pretty, huh?"

"That don't matter. Take her through the back."

"She goes where we go."

"Through the back, man."

"Goodbye, man. We get back in our bus and you tell all the shit kickers coming to this barn to spend their money, that Bobbi Mercer ain't here because she wouldn't go through the back."

"Look, it ain't me."

"Me neither."

"Bring her in, hurry up."

* * *

Through the forties and into the fifties, Patsy Cogootz would not be far from songs. If he couldn't hear them, he sang them — wailed some of the string and horn lines too, and the rhythm sections.

Sometimes all the radios in the house made music. A small one in the music room, one in his bedroom, or the big one in the living room, where he sat, fingertips on the tuning knob, eyes on the lighted dial, finding one particular sound from way out in Cleveland. Songs drifted in, faded, came back. Records with growling saxophones, heavy back beats, men's voices in heartbreak harmony that he and the other guys would be singing under the schoolyard stoop on the day Red Vest took a header onto the ash cans.

Like mob guys, they never talked about things like Red Vest. But Charlie Fish and Vinny Blond never stopped arguing about an end to the neighborhood. They got the big Cogootz boo-hooing to his mother about it, who told him that as long as his songs came from his heart, the neighborhood would thrive.

His father told him the same thing, and wonder jumped to wide-eyed certainty for Cogootz. He told Charlie and Vinny and Mike about it. But when harmony under the stoop got real tight, Mike got drafted, the group broke up and Cogootz almost did too.

But then he got the job, thanks to his father and the *Mezzogiorno* guys, at the Patarama Funeral Parlor, keeping the halls and parlors and embalming room clean. And with sadness and grief all around him, he never let the songs stop, and the songs, at least for a while, didn't allow the dead to die. Really die.

Pablo Picasso Does the Right Thing for Philomena

After days of discussion, Philomena and the saints agreed to deliver Don Camillo's dinner and bring the painting that had been in the hatbox under her bed. The priest, the number of his years evasive beneath quick eyes and snappy moves, listened as he finished a pork chop with potatoes and *rapini*.

After dinner, with saucers of ice cream and cups of coffee on the table, and Philomena looking on, he wrote to the Archdiocese of New York.

He believed, he wrote, that a devoted and trustworthy parishioner, "has come into contact with an early version of Picasso's *Blind Man's Meal,* of which I know little, but understand that it has been missing from the Church, specifically from Barcelona's Cathedral of the Holy Cross, since the beginning of the century, and that its worth is not measurable."

He went on: "But for the consideration that includes no request for money, but a reward valuable only to this parishioner, will assure a return of the painting to the Church."

Phone calls and meetings, inspections, appraisals and agreements followed before Don Camillo, Philomena and the saints pulled Father Laurio Matruzzo from a small parish in upstate New York, where they called him Father Louie, to

Christ the King Church, where he got his name back, never learned how he got there, but lived pleasantly among the good people of the neighborhood.

Charlie Fish Gets Whacked

A Saturday night in September, 1983, the lacy patterns of small white lights arched the street for the opening night of the Feast of San Gennaro. Women sat at their windows watching their neighbors place bets at gambling wheels, crowd food stands for sausage, calzones and zeppoli, or crabs and shrimp.

Behind a pastry stand, a lady with sprays of powdered sugar on her nail polish chuckled under her white apron and called: "Look, look. Look at them here! How many you want, signora? And you, Charlie, how many?"

Charlie Fish Tonno, locked in a cluster of people walking slowly, smiled, shook his head no, and continued, stopping for a smile and a gander at the young girl behind a jewelry counter. Where the crowd thinned, he met up with Fat Cosmo, out on bail on a New Jersey hijacking case.

"Cosmo, hang around," Charlie Fish said. "I'll be right back."

"Where you going?"

"Gotta see about a call. Wait for me."

"Heard about Vinny Blond?"

"I'll be back."

The strings, horns and cymbals on the bandstand climbed into an up tempo, and Fish marched from the bright streets of the feast into a side street shaded by a line of old trees.

Father Laurio had just missed him. He had been walking, humming with the band and speaking with ladies who, as young mothers, had known his mother. They told him, as they'd told him so many times before, of being in the church during Mass on the San Gennaro feast day, when she'd fallen dead.

"She had a smile on her face."

"She didn't suffer."

"She prayed so hard for you to come to Christ the King."

He neared the edge of the feast.

"Going home already, Father?" a man called.

"Mass in the morning," he called back. "Maybe you should come."

"Glass of wine?"

"Tomorrow night maybe."

"And get us some rain," the man said, and lightning ripped through the black sky.

"Looks like it's here," Father Laurio said, looking at the sky and stepping into the same dark that Charlie Fish had entered. The sounds of the feast softened as he walked to the churchyard's gate, onto a brick walk and up two stone steps to the vestibule door. He shouldered the door open just as the rain broke, its sharp rattle on the slate roof nearly hiding the crack of a gunshot.

But he'd caught that sound, let it go as a firecracker, till two more shots took him to a rear window in the rectory. He picked up the phone on his desk.

"What is your emergency?"

"This is Father Matruzzo, Christ the King Church. I heard shots and saw someone running from our schoolyard. I think someone is on the ground."

"Describe the runner?"

"Black raincoat."

"That's it?"

"That's all."

He snatched an umbrella and hoofed through the rain to where a bare bulb above the schoolyard stoop cast a circle on a man on the ground, his left knee angled sharply, its foot tucked under the other knee. The elbows held angles too, so did the wrists, at the waist like the paws of a sleeping dog.

Thick head of hair, black going white. White shirt, a fold of money half in, half out of its pocket, and tan pants. On a neck chain, a San Gennaro medal. Father Laurio had blessed that medal — 18 karat, made in Italy, he remembered. It and the face with three pink holes in it, belonged to Charlie Fish Tonno.

Rain slowed and minutes passed when a police car bounced through the schoolyard gate and stopped, headlights on the body. The cops got out.

"Was it you who called, Father?"

"Yes." Laurio folded shut his umbrella.

"We got a black raincoat. Nothing further?"

"He ran out that gate."

One cop got on the radio, the other took traffic cones and yellow tape from the trunk.

A black Plymouth slid in, stopped behind the first police car. Two detectives, one of them with his suit jacket open and stressed at the shoulders, pants crimped at the waist and bagged at the knees, was Mike Mazzi.

"You called this in, Laurio?"

"It's Charlie, Mike. Charlie Fish."

"No shit."

Mike and his partner, Jim Conroy, quick, tall, young, flanked the body. They looked and pointed, stooped and examined. Mike took the money from Charlie's shirt pocket, handed it to Conroy.

"You heard three shots, Laurio?" Mike asked.

"Yes, three."

"Something about a raincoat?"

"Somebody in a black raincoat ran out the gate and that's all."

"Man, woman, black, white?"

"I don't know."

"Anything else?"

"That's all I saw from that window." Father Laurio pointed.

"You okay?" Mike asked.

"I'm okay. Can I anoint the body."

"Think he cares?"

"He will soon."

※ ※ ※

Sunday morning. No sleep, no shower, no shave, cardboard coffee cups on the dashboard.

Sammy Pepe, a skinny man with big ears and lonely strands of gray hair, had been stepping in and out of the *Mezzogiorno Social Club*, as San Gennaro watched from the window.

Inside, men playing cards, drinking coffee, looked up when Mike and Jim walked in behind Sammy.

"Hello, Sammy," Mike said.

Sammy turned. "Hey, Mike, how you doing?"

"Good, Sammy."

"Madonn', you look more like your father every time I see you."

"Yeah, that's what they say. Listen, we gotta talk to Dominic. He's here?"

"Yeah, he don't stay home no matter what. He figured you guys would be around. I was just looking out for you. I'll go get him — oh, here he is."

Dominic Tonno stepped from the kitchen. Nothing about him looked like he might be Charlie Fish's father except his hair, full and wavy, bright white. Too many pounds, but solid, filled the white knit shirt. The same kind of shirt his son had worn to his murder.

The detectives stood, Mike introduced Jim.

"Michael, just like your father you look. How's your mother?"

More grit had accumulated in Tonno's voice since the last time Mike heard it.

"She's good."

"Good. Sit down."

They all sat at a table behind San Gennaro.

"Sorry about Charlie," Mike said.

"Yeah, thanks."

"We have to talk about it."

"I figured."

"Anything you could tell us, any problems?"

"Problems all the time. Stick ups, husbands, fathers, forget about it. If he woulda behaved, he coulda had the world by the *cogliones*." Tonno looked at Jim, back to Mike.

"Any problems lately?" Mike asked.

"Not that I know, but you could bet he was making some." Tonno almost yelled, sounded annoyed. "He was fucking everything. He didn't care who, whose wife, nothing."

"How's your wife doing? Your daughters?"

"My daughters are doing good. My wife, what could I tell you?"

"We could use help."

Dominic Tonno shrugged, held it. "For you I do what I could, Michael." He let go the shrug. "Within reason. Hey look, the black car. You're getting a ticket. They give you guys tickets?"

"Cops ain't what we used to be, Dominic."

"Fucking meter maids."

"Jim, make sure we don't get banged," Mike said.

"Yeah, sure."

Jim scooted out, Mike leaned, looked around the San Gennaro statue, watched Jim make the meter maid smile.

"How old are you now, Mike?" Tonno asked.

"Forty two."

"Sure, like my son."

"How old are you, Dom?"

"Social Security. Michael, look. I don't know who whacked my son. Nobody came to me with a problem. You understand?"

"Three in the face," Mike said.

"Don't sound like business."

"Anything about it mean something?"

"Only what I said. Husbands, fathers, jealous fucking women. I find out something, then two things could happen. Either we tell you, or we don't, but you'll figure it out."

***

Mike ducked into the Plymouth.

"Anything?" Conroy asked.

"Cooperation."

"Yeah?"

"He's says he's gonna find out who killed his son."

"Then what?"

"He's gonna whack him. Let's go eat."

Jim moved the Plymouth, stopped at a light.

Mike rolled down his window. "Cogootz," he called out.

"Aye, Mikey, aye, Mikey." Cogootz waved a long arm, threw a shiny grin.

"This is the guy I told you we want to see," Mike said to Conroy. "From the funeral parlor."

Jim pulled to the curb near the schoolyard, a softball game, a hundred spectators looking through the tall chainlink fence.

Mike and Jim got out of the car, stood near the fence, waited for Cogootz to cross the street.

"This guy's still in the fifties," Mike said. "Look at him."

Old jeans, clean, rolled cuffs, faded black t-shirt, pack of cigarettes in its small pocket, feet in black leather shoes, a bony hand at the Yankee cap on his head.

Still crossing, Cogootz called: "Hi Mikey. What are you, working now? On Sunday?"

"Gotta keep guys like you out of trouble. Get outta the street."

Cogootz strode past Mike and Jim, looked in the Plymouth's side window. "You got a police radio and a regular radio too."

"Told them I don't work on Sunday unless I could tune in the Doowop Shop."

"You didn't say that. They'd say up your giggy."

"How you doing?" Mike asked.

"Something about Charlie, huh?"

"How's your wife, your daughter?"

"Good."

"How old is she now?"

"My wife?"

"Your daughter."

"Sweet sixteen. Something about Charlie, huh? Think the neighborhood is gonna end now, with no more Charlie Fish?"

"You serious?"

"Yeah."

"As long as we could sing, we got no problem," Mike said.

"That's what we used to say. Remember?"

"I remember."

"But years now we don't hit harmony."

"You know all the parts. You could sing them, one at a time."

"Come on, Mikey. You know that ain't the same."

"But it's good enough." Mike stepped, turning to Jim. "Patsy, this is my partner, Jim Conroy."

"Hello Patsy, glad to meet you."

"You could call me Cogootz, Jim." He stuck out a hand. Jim's hand got lost in it.

"Something about Charlie, huh?" Cogootz said again.

"You shake Jimmy's hand, you don't shake mine?"

"Oh, yeah." Cogootz grabbed Mike's hand. "Charlie sang great bass, right Mikey?"

"Great bass. What do you know about what happened?"

"With Charlie? I don't know nothing. Father Laurio saw the guy, ask him."

"How you know that?"

"Everybody knows. But I know who Father Laurio saw. I mean, I bet."

"Who?"

"You know who."

"Who?"

"What everybody says."

"Who?"

"Don't make me say. I ain't going to say."

"Cogootz, it's me. Who?"

"Cosmo."

Cheers from the schoolyard made the three men look through the chain link fence, runner rounding first, going for second.

"He around?"

"He was at the feast last night. Nobody says they seen him, because he's the guy who killed Charlie and they don't wanna say."

"Okay, hold on. When did you last see Charlie?"

"Two, three weeks ago, going in the club, but I didn't talk with him."

"What about before that?"

"I don't remember."

"Why would Cosmo want to kill Fish?"

"Because he's a fat bastard."

"How long since he's been around?"

"Since I seen him last."

"When was that?"

"Two, three weeks ago, going in the club, but I didn't talk with him."

"That's what you said about Charlie."

"Yeah. Him and Charlie. Hey, hey, hey. Mike the cop's grilling his friend. Don't give me a beating, Mikey, huh?" Cogootz ducked make believe head shots.

"What about Vinny? What's he doing?"

"Vinny don't come hardly around no more. Neither do you." Cogootz folded his arms over the pack of cigarettes in his shirt pocket. "We all used to be together. And you know, Mikey, this new music ain't shit."

"I know."

"Well, I gotta go to work. Hey. You know Charlie's name is really Carmine?"

"Yeah, we knew that. His grandfather was Happy Carmine."

"Yeah, now I remember. Happy Carmine."

"Yeah."

"Okay, gotta go to work, see what Charlie's got to say. Get it, see what Charlie's got to say?"

Mike said: "He says anything good, you call me."

"Okay, Mike. See ya."

"If *anybody* says anything good, call me."

❊ ❊ ❊

Cogootz went through the alley to the back stairs of the Patar-ama Funeral home, pushed open the door into the preparation room, and stepped to the cadaver of Charlie Tonno.

"What's up, Cogootz?" Charlie Fish didn't sound sad, or afraid.

"Hi, Fish. Well, good to see you." Cogootz shot Fish with a finger. "Somebody got you, huh?"

"Cogootz, why'd you kill me?"

"Me? Get outta here. Why would I do that? And I'm a jerk off anyway. Remember what you used to call me?"

"Yeah, well, I don't know about you now, the way you could imitate everybody, like for a sneaky reason or a joke or something."

"How do you know I'm imitating everybody? Maybe it's really them talking."

"Yeah, right. Anyway, it ain't so bad being fucking dead. I'm still Charlie Fish."

"Yeah, but Charlie Fish, pretty soon in the dirt and the worms. Wanna hit some harmony?"

Vinny Blond, Hit Man

Young Joseph Petrosino's hook into the Detective Bureau was his name. Lieutenant Joe Petrosino, boss of the famous Italian Squad, was his uncle, his grandfather's brother. The young Joseph Petrosino, tall and slim, light brown hair, ten years on the job, works in the Organized Crime Control Bureau. That's where Mike Mazzi calls him.

"You're calling about the Tonno homicide," Joe says. "We just got your paperwork."

"Yeah, but first I'm talking about Vinny Biondi. Vinny Blond. You know him."

"Hit man."

"You're looking at him for a homicide?"

"A few homicides," Joe said.

"Tommy Benalatto of them?"

"That's not yours too, is it?"

"No, but it's why Vinny called me."

Mike says that Biondi hit Tommy Benalatto, but was supposed to hit Tommy's brother, Lenny. With the guy who put out the hit looking for him, Vinny figures he's gonna get whacked, doing time can't be worse, maybe catch a break by turning on some people. They set up a meet.

***

Mike and Joe at the entrance to the DA's office, Biondi's late, must have changed his mind, or maybe he got clipped already. But he shows up in ironed jeans, a suede sport jacket, and a blond rug on his head. He's slim, wiry and fidgety, and looks younger than fifty-three. The three shake hands. Mike gives Biondi a paper bag.

"What's this?" Biondi asks.

"Lunch."

They get to a file room on the fourth floor, Mike closes the door, kicks up dust. They sit around a three legged desk, and Biondi opens up like talk radio. About hits, who set up the contracts, where the guns, the silencers came from. Stuff they know, stuff they didn't know. Like with Tommy Benalatto.

"Benalatto," Mike says. "Run through that again."

"You know this shit ain't easy."

"Yeah, you're all choked up," Mike says. "Me too."

Biondi picks up his sandwich, stuffs his mouth, takes a minute. "What is this, horse cock?" He puts the sandwich in the bag it came in, sips soda.

"You still live in the neighborhood, Mike?" he asks.

"Yeah."

"Still married?"

"Yeah. You?"

"Seen my wife lately?"

"No," Mike says.

"You remember her?"

"Sure. From the projects. Nilda, Puerto Rican kid, real pretty."

"Get a look at her now."

"How many kids?"

"Four."

"Well, what do you expect?"

Vinny Blond asks Joe: "You from the neighborhood?"

"Used to be, yeah."

"You remember us singing?"

"In the schoolyard, in the hallway, on the corner. I was a kid."

A half minute goes by, the three guys looking at one another.

"Your mother and father, the fruit stand," Mike says to Biondi, "I don't see anymore. They still with us?"

"My mother, yeah."

"Who whacked Charlie Fish?"

"Smooth move, Mikey," Vinny Blond says and laughs. "Nice try."

Mike laughs. "Who whacked him?"

"I don't give a fuck about Charlie Fish, and Koreans got the fruit store."

"Dominic gonna do something about it?"

"The Koreans?"

"The hit."

"I know, I'm breaking balls. I don't hear nothing about that."

"Tell us what happened with Tommy."

"You knew him?"

"No," Mike says.

Vinny Blond leans in his chair, says: "All right," sips from the can of soda, sits back. "I go up the apartment, I got a box of *pignoli* cookies — they told me he likes them — and an envelope that I make sure he sees."

"Where'd you get the cookies?"

"Up the Bronx, make it hard for you guys."

"Anybody with you?" Joe asks Vinny.

"Nobody."

"No driver?"

"Alone."

"Go ahead."

"He answers the door, he's in a bathrobe. He looks like he don't know me, because he don't, and he says, 'Yeah' and I say, 'It's me, Vinny. They told me to bring you something.' Who told you, he wants to know, then he sees the envelope — looked like he wasn't expecting it — which now I know was for the brother, but he takes it and sticks it in a pocket of the bathrobe. I put the cookies on the kitchen table, he starts making black coffee, tells me get the anisette from a shelf."

Biondi's eyes look flat and black, but it looks like he's gonna laugh. He shifts in his chair.

"He's drinking, I'm drinking the coffee, I get up like to go take a leak, look around, make sure nobody else is there. I go back in the kitchen, he's sitting at the table, counting the bills from the envelope. All hundreds. I'm looking at his back, I take out the gun. Twenty-two."

"Revolver? Automatic?" Joe asks.

"Revolver. You know that."

"Silencer?"

"Yeah."

"Go ahead."

"I put one behind his ear. He falls over on the table, coffee and anisette all over the fucking place. Hundred dollar bills from the envelope. But he ain't dead. This fucking guy ain't dead. He's sitting, gasping like, looking at me, like. Ah, fuck."

Vinny lifts himself off the chair, gets into a stoop, falls back in the chair like he's tired.

"I don't wanna shoot again, I shouldn't even be there now. But the silencer is shit, a noisy fucking thing. I go pee for real, come back, he ain't dead. What am I gonna do? I make more coffee. I'm eating *pignoli* cookies and drinking coffee and now he's dead, and that's that."

"Go on," Joe says.

Vinny shrugs. "I felt bad, I mean, I didn't want him to suffer, I didn't even want to hit the fucking guy. He never did nothing to me. Lenny, who I'm thinking this is, never did nothing to me either." Shrug. "Fucking shitty silencer. I wonder ..."

"You wonder what?" Mike says.

"If he knew the cookies weren't for him either."

A minute of quiet, nobody talks, Vinny coughs a few times.

"Why'd they want him hit?" Joe asks.

"Not for me to know," Vinny Blond says.

"Why the envelope?"

"Far as I know, to give me a reason to be there. I was supposed to leave it, make sure you guys know it wasn't a stick up. I took it. A grand, what the fuck? Throw it away?"

"Who clipped Charlie Fish?" Mike asks.

"I don't know. But this guy you should clip."

"What guy?" Mike asks.

"The guy that gave you this fucking sandwich. Where'd you get this fucking thing?"

"The neighborhood."

"In the old days he woulda caught a beating with a sandwich like this. You know, the old days, when we ran things."

"Who runs things now?" Joe asks.

"Dominic makes a good boss for the newspapers and for the FBI when they gotta get in the newspapers. All bullshit now, cause there's nothing to run when you got a neighborhood choking, like on its last breath."

Mike says: "You still with that?"

"The end of the neighborhood?"

"Yeah."

"I was right when we were kids, and I'm more right now. If you guys look you could see that we're on a deathbed. Just look." He looks at Joe. "People used to pay to get into this neighborhood. Think they would now? Been to the feast? Everybody but Italians selling sausages and cotton candy and all that. This free hole mayor we got brings them in. Ever get a fucking arab *calzone*? Go to the club, Gennaro in the window. Poor guy cries when there's the feast."

Biondi grabs his sandwich bag, tosses it in a waste basket.

"Used to be good, Joe. Mikey knows. Fucking shame. All the things everybody did to keep it good. This fucking thing that I don't know how you could even call it a neighborhood. You know what I'm saying, Mikey. Same thing Lina's been saying for who knows how many years."

"You seen her?" Joe asks.

"You know her?" Vinny Blond asks.

"I know who she is."

"She's getting out, you know," Vinny Blond says.

"Where's she going?" Mike asks.

"The next century or something like that. Fucking midget's a mystery."

"She's already gone, I hear," Joe says, and Mike looks at him.

"Figures," Vinny Blond says. "And you know why?"

"I know what I hear, but you tell me," Joe says.

Biondi looks to Mike, says: "What I been saying? The neighborhood goes, she goes."

"Yeah, you been saying."

"She wanted us to keep this neighborhood. She was almost crying to my mother. The way it used to be. Even with hits and broken legs, nobody caught a beating who didn't have it coming. Taking care of ourselves. No locked doors, your mother, your grandmother, your sister were safe. Now its purse snatches, burglaries, piss on the streets. And if you kill one of these fucks," he looked at Mike here, held a beat, "you guys look to lock us up. If Lina's gone, I ain't surprised, and I don't fucking blame her."

"What about you?" Mike asks. "You did nothing to make her go?"

"I did crimes, I did sins. But I did what I was put here to do. I went with it. Just like her, she knows that. Just like you guys."

"How do you know you were put here to do hits?"

"It just happened, started years back with a guy with a red vest. Just happened. You know what I mean, Mikey."

"I know, yeah. And Lina's good with that?"

"She ain't good with guys getting clipped. None of that shit. But she knew the story. She was like us, I mean you do what you were put here to do. Sometimes you don't know what it is, till you're in the middle of something. Take the good with the bad, and make no calls on it. Like we all got a purpose or something. Lina always said that. Even before."

"Before what?"

"Before there was the neighborhood. Before the church, the stores, the buildings, before everything here."

"How you know that?"

"She says. And my grandmother used to say too. Since before she knew my grandfather, when she was still a little girl, she knew Lina. You live that long and you ain't a normal fucking midget, you know."

Joe says to Mike: "My Uncle Joe talked with her about the Black Hand, the letters, the bombs, the kidnaps, the murder stable, all those stories."

"Yeah, see?" Biondi says.

"She helped him find the bodies in the stable before the place burned down. He almost didn't go to Palermo because of what she told him. If he listened to her ... But he told my father—like Vinny says—he had to do what he had to do, and told my father to take care of his wife while he was gone."

"He knew he wasn't coming back," Vinny Blond says. "Lotta balls. A cop, but a lotta balls."

Vinny Blond and the detectives made quick eye contacts.

"I don't know what he knew, but he was worried," Joe says. "But more worried not to do the right thing—the right thing for the neighborhood. He liked his picture in the paper, yeah, everybody knows, but he did the right thing for a lot of people."

"And now forget about it. It's all over," Vinny Blond says, his hands thrown up. "Nothing to show for it."

Cogootz to the Rescue

The guys called him Fat Cosmo and Butter Ass; the kids called him Waddle; the girls called him Animal. His father, in Downstate Prison, which was upstate, probably forgot his name. But, Emilia, the good woman who was his mother, called him Cosmo, or sweetheart, or mostly, my son.

She'd been praying for years, but she knew there was no way her son couldn't go bad. For years he'd seen her catch beatings from her husband, a dock worker, built the same way as his son. Home after a few stops and a few snorts, he'd play a game with Cosmo, slapping Emilia around, making the four-year-old — then the five- and six-year-old — help out with kicks and punches for rewards of ones, fives and tens.

She still called him my son, and she still worried for him when he left the neighborhood for months, even years at a time, no mail, no phone calls.

On a Sunday morning she dressed right up to her small brown hat with the short veil, and sat in the kitchen, a cup of espresso and a biscuit, and the Italian station on the radio.

When it got time to leave for Mass, she washed and dried the coffee cup, put it away, took her purse and, on the way out, near the front door, saw her son's duffle bag.

"Oh, look, I didn't even hear him come in," she mumbled, a smile in her chest. She tiptoed to his room, cracked open the door, saw him sleeping, and took a container of frozen sauce out of the freezer.

She was at Mass when the cops knocked on her door, rang the bell, heard nothing but a macaroni commercial on the Italian station. One of the cops walked around the house talking to the radio in his hand.

"Sector Eddie to Central."

"Go ahead, Eddie."

"Got a caller on that DOA?"

"Anonymous male caller is all we got."

"Ten-four."

At the back of the house the cop looked through an open window, saw a fat man in a bed under a sheet, a gun on the floor just inside the window.

* * *

Mike Mazzi filled out the form in the Ballistics Unit: *Smith and Wesson, Military and Police, .38; holster wear, bluing off the barrel.* He had called the Records Section with the serial number.

"Got an owner," the cop at Records said.

"Go ahead."

"Ernest Baci, Police Officer, retired from the Three-One Precinct in nineteen-seventy-two. Deceased."

"Got a date on the death?"

"Call Pensions."

"Address?"

"Best get that from Pensions too."

The Ballistics detective held the gun. "Cop's gun, huh?"

"Yeah."

"He the shooter?"

"Doesn't look that way."

* * *

Back in the squad room, Mike got a call.

"Mazzi."

"Yeah, Mike, I was at the club last night."

"Yeah, Cogootz."

"They were saying that Cosmo killed Fish."

"I thought they been saying that all along."

"Yeah, but now they're whispering and shit like that. You know what I mean."

"When?"

"Last night."

"What did you hear?"

"Saying things like the cops'll be all over the neighborhood because of this fat fuck."

"Did they say his name?"

"No. They always call him fat fuck."

"Hear anything else?"

"No."

"Where are you now?"

"Home."

"Anything else?"

"You know what I found?"

"No, what?"

"A whole bunch of tapes. The Cleftones, The Ravens, The Harptones, The Heartbeats. I'll let you hear them sometimes if you want. The Eldorados, The Flamingos. I mean you could come here, or I'll lend them to you if you want."

"Yeah, good," Mike said.

"But you gotta be careful with them. And you know what else?"

"What?"

"Remember we used to practice in my music room up the stairs?"

"Yeah."

"There's tapes of that too. Of us. We were good, man."

"Hear about anything else today?"

"No."

"About Cosmo?"

"No, what?"

"He's dead."

"Dead? Where's he dead?"

"In his bed. During the night, shot while he was sleeping."

"Holy shit. When, today?"

"During the night."

"Holy shit. See, I told you he killed Charlie."

"Yeah, you did."

"Hey, Mike."

"Yeah."

"Did he still have that fifty-seven Chevy?"

***

The Pension Section gave Mike a phone and an address for retired cop Ernest Baci in a north Bronx neighborhood. Jim Conroy called, set up a visit.

A short, trim woman with soft white hair and thick glasses answered the door.

"Mrs. Baci?" Conroy asked.

"Yes, come in." The woman's voice was light, patient. She

yawned. "Oh, excuse me. We got in at two this morning from a wedding. I didn't even go to church. Come and sit."

Walking into the kitchen, Conroy said: "You're tired, we won't be long."

"We're sorry about your husband," Mike said.

"Thank you. He was a smoker. I threw out all the ash trays. I hope you men don't smoke."

"No, we don't smoke."

They sat at the kitchen table.

"These weddings," Mrs. Baci said, "music so loud, you can't even talk. Next time I'll send an envelope and stay home. Do you have time for coffee?"

"No thank you, we need to get back," Mike said. "We're interested in your husband's service gun."

"Oh yes?"

"As far as we know, he only had that one gun. He sold another one when he retired."

"His off duty he sold, I think, because the gun he kept was the gun he carried every day for thirty-four years and wouldn't feel right without it."

"Do you know where it is now?" Mike asked.

"Well, I hope so. He wanted it buried with him."

"Buried with him? In the coffin?"

"Well, yes."

"Where was he laid out?" Mike almost shouted.

"Patarama. All the family are still down the old neighborhood."

❈ ❈ ❈

Thunder rumbled as Mike and Jim got out of the Plymouth. Darkness clicked on the feast's lights and bandstand music funneled into the Patarama alley. At a basement window tilted open, they stopped and stooped to look down into the prep room. Five cadavers under white sheets lay on gurneys parked in a loose circle.

Cogootz, his Yankee cap at the back of his head, earphones draping his neck, skated the mop across the floor in careful arcs.

"So they made fun of me and goofed on me, and thought I was a jerk," somebody was saying. "But I'm not stupid."

"Yes, you're stupid," a man's voice said.

"No, you're stupid," Cogootz snapped. "And you got shot because you're a rat bastard."

The detectives scanned the prep room for the other man, found no one. In another room maybe.

Then the voice said: "You talk with the dead, and I'm stupid?"

The voice ran a chill through Mike. It sounded like Cosmo.

"Yeah, I talk with the dead. So what? First of all, they ain't dead. I see to that. And they got a lot to say, and they don't like you either. Nobody likes you, fat boy."

"But I gotta hand it to you, you fooled the whole fucking neighborhood."

"Well, that means I ain't stupid," Cogootz said.

"And you think you're a hero because you got away with murder."

Mike's and Conroy's faces, tinted green by the fluorescence from the window, looked at each other, then watched Cogootz swing the gurneys out of the way of his mopping.

"It means I'm smart."

"Yeah, real smart," the voice said.

A woman's voice butted in: "Leave him alone! He's smart, look what he did. Gave them what they deserved."

"Be quiet," Cogootz said. "I mean, not so loud, Mrs. Lodiccio. Please. Somebody might hear."

"Sorry," Mrs. Lodiccio said.

"That's okay," Cogootz said. "You shouldn't have to hear all this. I saw your daughters before. They were crying like I cried when my mother came here."

"Oh, no, I feel so bad. Please tell them, Pasquale, that it's not what they think, that I'm doing fine."

"I can't do that, Mrs. Lodiccio."

"Oh, please."

"I start talking like that and right away they think I'm *patso*. It would do no good, believe me. Your daughters will be all right."

Cogootz shut his eyes, as if to keep from saying too much. "Anyway, I had a talk with Fish, that son of a bitch, and he admitted everything."

"Of course he admitted everything," Mrs. Lodiccio said. "He don't want to go to hell, where he belongs."

"Yeah, well, that's where he's going. Pray for him, okay, but that's where he's going."

A damp wind whipped around a corner of the building, the detectives shifted their backs to it.

Cogootz got back to the mop, backed himself into a gurney and nudged it against a wall. "Why are you crying, Mrs. Gannon?"

"I worry for the neighborhood, you know, the schoolyard murder and all."

"Yeah, I know what you mean. But it's gonna be okay. I'm here, so don't worry. As long as we got these songs" — he tapped the small tape player in his shirt pocket — "and as long as I can sing them, we got the neighborhood."

Cagootz beamed. He had become important. Soon the whole neighborhood would thank him.

"I hope you're right, Pasquale, but look how people are now. No one is decent to anyone anymore."

"You mean decent like it used to be?"

"Yes, kindness, love."

"I know what you mean," Cogootz said. "And you know what else?"

Cogootz pointed with his thumb. "That mountain over there? That's not a mountain. That's Fat Cosmo, a mean son of a bitch, never was nice to nobody, so nothing changed for him."

"Yeah," Fat Cosmo said. "But it was Fish who raped your daughter. Not me."

Cogootz stomped, a bull charging the massive cadaver. "Shut up, you fat animal." He pulled the sheet from Fat Cosmo's face.

Bent at the waist, his face inches above Cosmo's, he growled: "I told you never say that. I told you don't tell nobody." He stood straight, squared the Yankee cap on his head, sent his voice down an octave. "You coulda stopped him, scumbag."

"You don't know shit."

"Fuck you. I'm sorry for the language, Mrs. Lodiccio and Mrs. Gannon. I'm very sorry, but this guy. You know?"

"That's all right, Pasquale," Mrs. Lodiccio said.

"Yes, it is all right," Mrs. Gannon said. "You're a fine man. What you did, somebody should have done years ago."

"Thank you, ladies. Anyway, I hear everything, Fat Cosmo. That's why I know all the songs, all the parts, the words. Because I listen. I listen to how people talk, that's how I talk like them. Talk like you. It's jerks like you too important to listen."

"Listen, huh?" Cosmo snapped. "The neighborhood is headed out of the picture and you're mopping floors and singing doowop like a dimwit."

"I sing for the neighborhood, fatso, and my singing is

what's keeping it going. What did you ever do for the neighborhood?"

"Cogootz, did you kill me?"

"Nice try, fatso. You killed Fish, and his uncle had to do something about it."

"I didn't kill Fish, you did."

"Okay, yeah. But the neighborhood says you did it and got killed because you did it, and that's what counts."

"You were a rat, Cogootz. You talked to Mike."

"Yeah." Cogootz strutted now, slowly, mop dragging behind him. "And he believes me, because he knows I ain't a scumbag like you." He stopped and bent at the waist. "And let me tell you about Fish. The big brave Fish, tough guy. Scared shit when he seen me. You could see in his face he knew what was up. Then when he seen the gun, he says: 'Stop fucking around, man.' But he knew what was up. He was scared so stiff that he couldn't even fall when I shot him. Right in the head, but it took two more shots to get him down. With all his bullshit, he couldn't say shit."

"Don't you feel bad?" Cosmo asked.

"Why should I feel bad? You guys thought I'm stupid, but you can't be stupid and set up a guy with a phone call the way I did. He really thought he was gonna get laid and instead he got shot. And you know why I ain't stupid? Because I hear a lot of things in the club, Fat Cosmo. Lot of things in this room too. Got a lot up in here." He tapped the side of his head with a finger.

"Yeah, you know a lot, but nothing to help when you get caught that you killed me and Fish."

"Oh yeah?" Cogootz paced around Cosmo now, big hands folded behind him, powerful, confident. "A lot of people don't know what I got. And I ain't saying nothing even if they give me a going over, which Mike won't let them do, 'cause I ain't a scumbag. I just listen. Get what I mean? And I never let Fish rape nobody."

"Yeah, well, I didn't either."

"Lying sack of shit."

"No, I ... Cogootz, I'm sorry that I let Fish rape your daughter. Real sorry."

"Sorry because you gotta look God in the eye. You ain't sorry. Him and me know that."

"I am, I am. Look. My fifty seven Chevy, it's still in the garage, it's yours. Just say you know I'm sorry."

Cogootz stopped pacing, held the mop still, rocked from side to side. "Don't tease, Cosmo."

"Take it, just tell my mother you forgive me."

"Yeah, I'm gonna bother your poor mother now. Keep the Chevy, stick it in your giggy."

"Come on," Cosmo whined, "I got some old forty-fives too."

"Yeah, that you stole from me."

"Forgive me, man."

Cogootz squared the Yankee cap on his head, and threw the sheet back over Cosmo's face. Then he put on the earphones, bopped a bass line, segued to a baritone part, a tenor part, then the lead. He stayed there for a few bars, then danced the mop to the center of the room, opened his arms, and ended the song with a sweet and soaring falsetto.

Acknowledgments

Old mug shots, conversations of criminal conspiracies, and Susan Mahoney, who read what I wrote and let me know what I was thinking.

About the Author

Ercole Gaudioso had a thirty-four-year career in law enforcement: twenty years with NYPD and fourteen years with New York State's Organized Crime Task Force. While part of the Organized Crime Task Force, Gaudioso led the five-year investigation that resulted in the arrests of 40 Gambino Family members including John Gotti, Jr. Since retiring from law enforcement, Gaudioso has dedicated his days to singing, photography and writing. His essays, articles and photos have appeared in detective magazines. His short stories and photos have appeared in various literary magazines, including *Inkwell* and have received various awards in literary and photographic competitions. He has achieved a Masters in Writing from Manhattanville College in Purchase, New York, and an MFA in Professional Writing at Western Connecticut State University. *The Mezzogiorno Social Club* is his first published novel.

Printed in August 2017
by Gauvin Press,
Gatineau, Québec